Mary's Salvation

The Chronicles of Mary Magdalene

Steve Taylor

STCNC

Best
Sellers
The Chronicles of Mary
Magdelene Series

Mary's Salvation
The Illuminated Path
Jerusalem's Faith
Paul's Odyssey
Andrew's Adventures
Mary's Celestial Journey

In the Company
of Angels
John's Journey
Heaven's Warriors
Isabella's Divine Destiny

WRITTEN BY

Steve Taylor
Https://maryschronicles.online

Mary's Salvation

The Chronicles of Mary Magdalene

Steve Taylor

STCNC

This Book is dedicated to my dear friend Sharyn, this is for her and the other strong Christian women that without their support, the Christian religion would have been lost to Monasteries and Cathedrals .With the Divine support of the Holy Spirit and these women, Christianity flourished in homes and churches in every corner of the world.By recieving the Holy Spirit they helped fulfill the commandment of Jesus to spread the gospel to the four corners of the world

Prologue- Unveiling the Divine Tapestry

I n a world that seemed to have forgotten the deep spiritual currents running through it, a chain of miraculous events began to stir the modern consciousness. In this dynamic, transformative narrative, we find ourselves on a journey weaving through time, guided by the visionary glimpses bestowed upon Mary Magdalene, a luminary figure whose story was yet to be fully revealed and celebrated in the annals of religious history.

In the bustling heartbeat of the modern era, an event of profound spiritual significance was unfolding. A skeptical journalist, having embarked on a journey to unveil the mysteries enshrouded within the Gospel of Mary stumbles upon a series of miracles pointing towards a grand cosmic plan. Through the celestial guidance of Mary Magdalene, he begins to perceive the intricate tapestry of events that had orchestrated the golden age of spirituality humanity was transitioning into.

Determined to unravel the enigma surrounding Mary Magdalene's role in the formative years of Christianity, the protagonist finds himself immersed in a quest that transcends time and space. As he delves deeper into the annals of religious history, he discovers the pivotal role played by Mary in nurturing the early Christian communities.

In the hallowed corridors of the Vatican library, whispers of ancient secrets beckon him further into a world where the boundaries between the celestial and earthly realms blur. A journey to Jerusalem reveals the vibrant history of the Qumran settlement, a place that once echoed with the celestial symphonies of spiritual enlightenment and knowledge. Here, he learns about Mary's efforts to preserve the spiritual heritage of Jesus Christ, a Gospel that had harbored profound spiritual truths, and her role in fostering a haven of spiritual learning and growth.

As the narrative unfolds, the protagonist finds himself tracing the luminous pathways carved by Mary Magdalene as she embarked on a mission to spread the teachings of Jesus across different lands. In Gaul, she established a sanctuary of knowledge, where the celestial teachings resonated with profound wisdom. In Britannia, she laid the foundations of the first Christian churches and schools, igniting the flames of spiritual awakening in the hearts of many.

The journey continued to the mystical landscapes of Scotland, where Mary's radiant presence transformed the spiritual fabric of the land, fostering communities that echoed with the harmonious symphonies of celestial wisdom. In Hispania, her collaboration with the apostle James became a beacon of light, guiding the populace towards a golden age of spirituality.

Each account, steeped in historical and spiritual depth, weaves a rich tapestry that showcases Mary Magdalene's indomitable spirit and her contributions to the spiritual evolution of humanity. Through her life, a luminous narrative unfolds, showcasing the transformative power of divine love and grace.

As the protagonist finds himself at the culmination of his spiritual quest, a profound realization dawns upon him. The miraculous events, the visions, and the celestial guidance were all orchestrated by Mary Magdalene, who had been steering humanity towards a golden age of spirituality from the celestial realms.

Through her guidance, a new era was unfolding, where the divine feminine energy would resonate in harmonious symphonies with the celestial realms, fostering a world where love, unity, and celestial harmony would craft a luminous saga of cosmic significance.

With renewed conviction and a heart brimming with celestial gratitude, the protagonist steps into the world, ready to share the luminous narrative of Mary Magdalene with humanity. As the world stands at the threshold of a golden age, the stories of Mary Magdalene become a beacon of light, guiding humanity towards a future resonating with love, unity, and celestial harmony.

Introduction- The Awakening

Mary Magdalene awoke from the shroud of another indulgent night, in the depths of worldly pleasures and sensuous enchantments. These pleasures, once alluring and intoxicating, had become an unsatisfying veil of deception, a trap binding her to the material world. Her life had become a vortex of vice and emptiness, the darkness engulfing her, alienating her from her own self. And yet, amidst the shadows, she felt a strange stirring. A dream a vision, perhaps was kindled in her somber slumber. In her dream, she saw a figure striding down the dusty streets of her town, an aura of tranquility around him, as though he walked not upon the earth but in a realm of divine grace. He had an otherworldly presence, and yet, he was so profoundly human. His eyes were filled with infinite compassion, the love radiating from him washing over the people around. It was Him Jesus Christ, the Son of God. She awoke with a start, the image of Jesus burned in her mind. His figure lingered in her thoughts, a beacon of hope piercing her darkness. The clarity was astounding she knew what she had to do. She had to find Him, beg for His divine grace, and plead for the salvation only He could offer. Armed with newfound resolve, Mary set forth on a journey. It wasn't an easy path the specter of her past life loomed in the shadows, ready to pull her back into the abyss. However, the Holy Spirit was with her, guiding her towards the divine path, inspiring her to chronicle the lives of the apostles after Jesus's ascension. Her journey was fraught with trials and temptations, the Devil weaving intricate webs of deceit to deter her from her spiritual path. Yet, Mary clung onto her faith, the joy of Jesus's salvation fueling her perseverance. This is Mary's tale, a tale of transformation from a life steeped in sin to a spiritual odyssey that intertwines with the paths of the apostles. An odyssey where the chains of her past are shattered, replaced by the divine light of the Savior's love. Are you ready to walk alongside Mary, witness her transformation, and explore the depth of her devotion to Christ? Join me as we delve into the untold story of Mary Magdalene and her extraordinary journey of redemption and spirituality. Let's turn the page to a chapter that defined an era and continues to inspire us to this day. Are you ready? Your spiritual transformation awaits Salvation Found Mary's journey to find Jesus was a pilgrimage of penance, a sincere search for redemption. Weary and worn, she sought Him through the winding streets of Jerusalem, her faith unwavering and her spirit undeterred. Finally, her persistence bore fruit. She found Him, preaching to a crowd, His words painting a picture of love, compassion, and salvation. His eyes met hers, and in that brief moment, Mary felt an overwhelming rush of understanding, acceptance, and forgiveness. He didn't see her past. He saw her heart. Her heart pounded in her chest as she fell to her knees at His feet, her eyes brimming with tears. She confessed her sins, baring her soul and the darkness that had resided within her for far too long. With a soft touch of His hand and a comforting look, He told her, "Your sins are forgiven." The sincerity and compassion in His voice were her absolution. As if washed clean by a divine spring, her sins were lifted from her. The dark veil of her past was torn away, replaced by a warmth that radiated from within, illuminating her entire being. It was an ecstasy she had never known the joy of salvation. With newfound faith and divine grace in her heart, Mary never returned to her former abode. Instead, she followed Jesus, devoting herself entirely to His teachings. Her belief was unshakable, her zeal unparalleled. She became one of His most ardent followers, spreading His message of love and forgiveness to everyone she met. As Jesus began to gather His apostles, Mary found herself in a special position. She wasn't just another follower she became a close confidant, a trusted friend. Jesus shared with her the profound mysteries of the new religion He was introducing to the world a religion of peace, compassion, and divine grace. It was a testament of love, a promise to bring humanity back into harmony with God, providing them the tools to triumph over the devil's machinations. Mary's transformation was truly miraculous. From a life shadowed by sin, she emerged a beacon of faith and hope. Her story was testament to Jesus's power of redemption and the divine potential within every soul willing to seek salvation. Mary's journey serves as a powerful reminder no matter how far one may stray, there is always a path to redemption for those willing to seek it. he Path of the Apostles As Jesus began gathering His apostles, Mary found herself in a unique position. Unlike the twelve who would be known throughout history, Mary's role was quieter, yet just as significant. She became the recorder of their journeys, a task given to her by the Holy Spirit. It was her mission to chronicle the lives and teachings of the apostles after Jesus's ascension. Mary moved in the apostles' shadow, observing their actions, their faith, and their struggles. Her pen seemed to be guided by an unseen hand, recording their travels and the expansion of the new religion. In her chronicles, Peter emerged as the steadfast rock upon which the early church was built. John, the beloved, etched himself in her narrative as a figure of profound love and wisdom. Thomas, the doubter, was a testament to honest and questioning faith. Each of the apostles, in their unique way, contributed to the burgeoning religion.

Yet, the journey was fraught with peril. The machinations of the devil were a constant threat, attempting to hinder their progress at every turn. But their faith remained unyielding. They met every challenge with courage and strength, their conviction a testament to their unwavering faith in Jesus. Mary chronicled each challenge and victory, her writings becoming a testament to their devotion. But Mary wasn't just a chronicler she was an integral part of their journey. Her presence was a constant source of comfort and strength to the apostles. She shared their burdens, rejoiced in their victories, and prayed with them in their darkest hours. In this spiritual journey, Mary became an apostle in her own right. Her former life seemed like a distant memory, a shadow from another lifetime. She was no longer a woman possessed by earthly desires she was now a vessel of divine love, an instrument of God's grace. Her journey of transformation was a beacon of hope for those living in darkness, a testament to the transformative power of Jesus's love. The joy of salvation was her constant companion, and she wore it like a shining armor, radiating a divine glow that touched everyone she met. In the midst of her mission, Mary found her true calling. She was a guide, a light illuminating the path for those seeking the divine grace she had found in Jesus. Through her words and deeds, she became a beacon of hope, a symbol of redemption, and an embodiment of divine love and grace. Mary's journey reminds us all it's never too late to seek redemption and discover your true purpose.

Chapter 1
Heaven's Gate

In a moment of divine brilliance, the Gate of Heaven split open. It was not merely an ethereal tear, but a celestial shattering, a rending of the fabric of the spiritual and physical realms. Unlike the gateways encountered by the prophets of the Old Testament, this was an event they described as the moment when God opened the gates of heaven by allowing His spirit to inhabit the physical realm as Jesus' divine spark. They had foretold it but had no idea of the glory of the opening of the veils between the two universes. One was the realm of God and His majesty; the other, the realm of men. Inhabited by God's shadow, thinking he was the Divine Creator, he had coerced Eve into eating from the tree of knowledge, causing the fall of mankind. This was much the same as the fall of angels spoken of in the Old Testament or the Jewish Torah. When the rift occurred, the Holy Spirit moved through it. As Jesus' spirit was returned to its place with God the Creator, it became the same divine spirit but now a "bridge" due to his physical manifestation and the manner of his death. It was not a mere path between two places. It was a break in the divine barrier, a passage that allowed the transcendent love of the Holy Spirit to pour into our world. Jesus, our beloved Teacher and Guide, had prepared us for this moment, yet the reality was more astonishing than we could have ever imagined. It was born out of an angelic invasion, an act of supreme sacrifice: His life for ours, His death for our salvation.

His ascension was a spectacle of divine wonder, a vision of serenity amid chaos. His figure, bathed in celestial light, rose, defying the pull of the earth. His last words still echoed in our hearts, "It is finished." With that, He surrendered Himself to the heavens, opening the path for the Holy Spirit. Mary, the mother, and I watched in awe as a surge of brilliant light exploded from the point where Jesus vanished into the clouds, and a torrent of divine energy burst forth. It was as if the sun had descended to bless the earth with an extraordinary light. Angels, figures of radiant light, emerged from the rift, their presence as reassuring as it was awe-inspiring. Each was a herald of His will, messengers assigned to aid the apostles in their divine mission. Their expressions were serene, their purpose firm, and their devotion to the cause unwavering. At the angel's behest, I began to document these miraculous occurrences. The angel explained, "Mary, your task is as crucial as the apostles'. You are to record these events: the opening of the gate, the descent of the Holy Spirit, and the subsequent journeys. You will bear witness to His word, His love, and His promise."

Chapter 2
The Devine Journey

M eanwhile, the apostles, filled with a strange yet exhilarating power, prepared to undertake their separate paths. Each apostle, a simple man transformed by divine intervention, seemed ready to embrace his fate. The divine mandate, heavy with responsibility, rested on their shoulders, with the whispers of the Holy Spirit guiding their every step. Peter, the rock of the Church, wore a determined look, his eyes resolute. John, the beloved, was calm, an oasis of tranquility amidst the brewing storm. James, fiery as ever, seemed ready to face any trial that lay ahead. Matthew, the tax collector turned disciple, had his trusty stylus and parchment ready to record the word of God.

As I conclude the account of this first miraculous event, I'm filled with a mixture of awe and anticipation. The stage is set, the players ready, and the journey about to begin. The road ahead is uncertain, filled with trials and triumphs. But with the guidance of the Holy Spirit and the protection of the angels, we are ready to venture into the unknown. The work of Salvation is about to begin.

However, even as the work commences, there is another who does not feel joy for these miraculous events. He is the Prince of the World.

His minions do his bidding, encouraging evil and misery into the realm of mankind. Determined to stop this miracle that God had set in motion, he sat in his shadowy kingdom, setting his machinations into play. His plans to deliver darkness to the Light that was invading his personal realm of misery were taking shape. The domination he planned for mankind, threatened by the rift caused by Jesus ascending into heaven, was causing him to rage. The minions of his realm were gifted with torturous, miserable gifts of his ire. They knew he would call on them to do his evil bidding, and until he did, they knew they would suffer. This made them all the more eager to set the Devil's plan into motion. Whatever he dreamed up sitting in his dark realm, they would ensure it happened in the realm of man. To fail was a guarantee of eternal misery. The Devil accepted no failure in his bidding of evil. His only emotion similar to joy was when he witnessed the pathetic creations of his original substance. He now knew he was the opposite in the universe, locked behind the veil that separated the heavens from the world. He considered himself a prince, albeit self-proclaimed. He ruled on this side of that veil. Yet, an opening had formed, and what had traveled into his realm was cause for great concern. This spirit was taking dominion over the souls in the middle realm, also known as the kingdom of mankind, inhabiting them and creating a block to his ability to influence them with his creation called the seven cardinal sins.

His resentment and jealousy created them in the moment he discovered he was not the supreme being of the universes, just a mirror of the real God of all the universe. In that moment, he succumbed to the jealousy of his newfound position. He had raged, and Pandora's box had been loosed on everything this side of the veil. He had cajoled Eve into eating from the tree of knowledge, causing the expulsion of the companions from God's fertile garden where they had lived in innocence. He removed them from God's grace and doomed mankind to be forever separated from God. This was the first of many treacheries he perpetrated on the sons to follow. God responded by choosing favorites from the population of mankind, endowing them with rules to live by, bound by commandments and rituals. These gifts he gave to the sons of Abraham, allowing them to receive cleansing from their sins and misdeeds. But the sons of men had no desire for the discipline of the rules and adopted the proliferation of the seven cardinal sins, his legacy. As he sat in his domain, the lowest level of what we consider the labyrinth of hell, he planned nonstop to corrupt the rules known as the Ten Commandments, delivered by one of God's favorites known as Moses.

Despite all his machinations, God had figured out how to interrupt the continuum and sent his spirit to dwell in the body of a man born of the flesh. This man, born of a virgin birth in the middle kingdom, had his spirit inhabit the body of the one known as Jesus. After Jesus' torture and death, he was resurrected. When he passed into heaven, a rift formed, and the Holy Spirit moved through into the middle realm, along with a horde of angels to protect the believers of Jesus' message. This caused a return to balance, overcoming his eons of planning to keep dominion over the middle realm. Now he had to replan all his strategies to stop the spread of this soul stealer, the Holy Spirit. This spirit would protect every soul that professed belief in Jesus' mission and the message he entrusted to a band of apostles and his companion and confidant, Mary Magdalene. He despised every one of them, but for her, he planned a special torment. He would use his minions to stop the growth of this new power that reversed his seven cardinal sins' hold on mankind, replacing it with morals, grace, forgiveness, and joy. He detested these attributes and refused to allow them in the realm of the middle kingdom. These attributes acted like a soul virus, causing his minions to be rejected as they tried to influence the inhabitants of the middle realm. This soul-restoring virus that God had sent in his grace was the way back to his divine presence. It was a gift of eternal joy versus the misery the devil spread over all the realms of the middle kingdom. The exact opposite of all he cared about. People could receive the blessing of the Holy Ghost and return to the heaven side of the veil, free from the sins that separated them from God's presence.

So, he sat in his dark shadow realm, despising everything related to the Apostles of Jesus Christ. But his hatred for Mary Magdalene, who had been thoroughly corrupted by the seven cardinal sins and was a dwelling for demonic spirits indulging in the sins of the flesh, was immense. He despised how, with just a touch, Jesus had instantly changed her into a warrior for his cause, fierce and now incorruptible, protected by an angel of the first magnitude. He imagined the despicable things in store for her when he again corrupted her fleshly shell, sending his demon to inhabit the flesh that was an abomination to his very sight. In his dark realm, he schemed.

Through the Devil's eyes, darkness swirled around him, a pool of simmering resentment and frustration. He, the self-proclaimed Prince of the World, observed from the shadows as the Son ascended, leaving the earthly realm behind. The air shimmered in His wake, and the light and warmth faded, leaving an uncomfortable emptiness that he intended to fill. The humans looked lost, their eyes reflecting a mix of sorrow and hope. Their hope was irritatingly infectious, gnawing at his insides. He hated it. He hated them. Their innocence was his downfall. The taste of the apple still lingered in his memory, a moment of victory that seemed so simple then. "Knowledge, the key to divinity," he whispered, leaving a poisonous promise hanging in the air. And they had taken it, their innocence crumbling with the bite of the fruit.

This fruit, which was meant to ensure their greatness, brought them nothing but pain.

Chapter 3
The First
Mission Begins

I t was an epoch unlike any other. With the ascension of Jesus and the descent of the Holy Spirit, an ethereal flame ignited within the apostles, embarking them on an extraordinary journey. This flame was more than an abstract idea; it was a tangible force that would guide their steps and enlighten their paths, making them emissaries of God's word. As I, Mary Magdalene, narrated the divine unfolding, I was filled with awe and reverence. In my private quarters, accompanied by an angel whose soft voice whispered the chronicles of heaven, I documented each extraordinary event.

Across the sprawling city of Jerusalem, an energy stirred. The apostles had embraced their mandate to spread the word of God and embody the teachings of Christ. Peter was the first to take his mission beyond Jerusalem, heading towards the coastal cities of Joppa and Caesarea. The rugged fisherman, once characterized by impulsiveness and fear, now exuded a divine authority that commanded respect and awe. In the bustling markets of Joppa, he shared Jesus' teachings, the love of God made manifest in Christ's sacrifice. His words flowed like a river, gentle yet relentless, drawing men and women to the shores of salvation. Meanwhile, John and James, the Sons of Thunder as Jesus fondly named them, ventured into Samaria. They preached with fiery zeal, their words striking like thunderbolts, inspiring awe, fear, and devotion among their listeners.

Even as the apostles commenced their divine duties, I stayed in Jerusalem, providing the female perspective of these divine events. I served as a spiritual pillar, leading women in prayer, guiding them in understanding Jesus' teachings, and ensuring they felt included in this divine mission.

The apostles' journeys were not without challenges. They were met with skepticism, fear, and sometimes hostility. But they never wavered, drawing strength from the Holy Spirit that filled their hearts, fulfilling their determination to carry out Christ's instructions. As I ended my chronicle for the day, I looked out at the city bathed in twilight. Somewhere out there, the apostles were making their way in the world, bringing light to the corners of the earth. And I, too, had my part to play, for we were all part of the great mission set forth by our Lord. The first mission had begun, the flame of the Holy Spirit guiding us towards a future of faith and salvation.

His eyes, burning with a malicious flame, observed the apostles as they began their mission. They moved with newfound purpose, a divine spark they had acquired from the Holy Spirit. As they treaded the familiar dusty roads, they now bore an air of unfamiliar conviction. The Devil watched intently as they split up, each heading to different lands. It amused him, their belief that they could face the world alone. Did they not comprehend the perils that awaited them? Were they so naive to believe that their words would be embraced universally? Or was it the newfound spirit that blinded them to the world's realities?

Peter, the rock upon whom the Son decided to build His church, marched towards Rome. The Devil's ghouls, he thought, had a special treat planned for Peter. Rome, a city engulfed in politics and pagan worship, was no place for a fisherman preaching about a carpenter's son. James was headed towards Spain, a land far from Jerusalem's familiarity. The Devil chuckled, imagining the locals' faces when James began preaching in tongues. Matthew chose to remain in Jerusalem, the faith's epicenter. This was a smart choice, the Devil mused. The soil there was fertile for the seed of the Holy Spirit. But even fertile lands needed tilling, and the Devil was ready with his plow of doubt.

The apostles had embarked on a seemingly impossible task. They appeared to be walking straight into a trap, like lambs led to slaughter. It seemed only a matter of time before they would realize the gravity of their situation. Mary Magdalene, he noticed, scribbled away, preserving the teachings of the Son and the events she had witnessed. The vigilant angel by her side caught the Devil's attention. He smirked, noting the determination in her eyes. She posed a challenge, but challenges were meant to be overcome. He would find a way.

As the Devil's minions spread across the land, sowing seeds of chaos and doubt, he took solace in the impending chaos. His minions had already started their work, whispering words of fear and uncertainty into the people's ears. They were adept at their craft. The apostles had begun their journey, a mission to spread love and hope. The Devil, too, had begun his mission—to ensure that their message drowned in a sea of doubt and fear. Their faith was undeniably strong, their resolve unwavering. However, the Devil was patient and time, he believed, was on his side.

Chapter 4
Shadows Stirring

In Jerusalem, I worked alongside Mary, mother of Jesus, navigating through complex societal structures to ensure the word of God was reaching everyone. We led prayer groups, taught parables, and became anchors for those overwhelmed by this tidal wave of divine change. Women, who were traditionally marginalized, found their voices, contributing significantly to this unfolding narrative of faith and redemption. Beyond our inner circle, other apostles ventured out on their individual missions.

Philip journeyed towards the Mediterranean, Bartholomew towards the northern regions, and Andrew towards the East. Each one experienced unique challenges, cultural differences, and varied responses to their message. Yet, the spirit of Christ's teachings united their diverse journeys. They were met with countless trials, from opposition by local religious leaders to threats from hostile communities, to personal challenges of doubt and fear. Yet, with each difficulty they encountered, their faith grew stronger. The more they leaned into the Holy Spirit for guidance, the clearer their paths became. These apostles, ordinary men transformed by the Holy Spirit, were reshaping the world. Their victories were not of the physical realm; they were spiritual triumphs. Hearts were being opened, lives were being changed, and the message of Christ's salvation was spreading like a divine wildfire.

As night fell on Jerusalem, I pondered over the prophecies of old and the unfolding reality. It all seemed divinely orchestrated, like a grand symphony playing out under the watchful eyes of heaven. Each apostle, each disciple, each convert was a note in this grand composition, contributing to a melody of salvation and grace. Our journeys had only just begun. As the apostles ventured forth to the ends of the earth, they carried with them the promise of God's kingdom and the hope of a new dawn for mankind. The apostles had started their missions in earnest, spreading the Gospel far and wide.

The Devil watched from the shadows, his eyes flickering with the dark thrill of the coming conflict. This was what he lived for: the chaos, the fear, the doubt – all instruments of his malevolent symphony. Peter, in Rome, found himself in the midst of the den of paganism. The people were more interested in their festivals, their gods, and their earthly pleasures. The Devil laughed as Peter tried to preach about salvation and spirituality to those whose minds were fixated on their next feast. He watched as Peter, filled with a righteous fury, was beaten and thrown out of the central square. It was a harsh lesson, but an important one. Rome would not be won over easily.

In Spain, James faced his own challenges. The language barrier was a minor issue, one that the Holy Spirit helped him overcome. But the real problem lay in the deeply ingrained beliefs of the locals. The Devil watched as James was laughed at, ridiculed for his strange stories. His message was like a pebble against a fortress, barely making an impact.

In Jerusalem, Matthew had a different kind of battle. He was preaching to those who had seen the Son with their own eyes, those who had heard His words firsthand. But they were skeptical, unwilling to believe that the man they had crucified was their Messiah. The Devil savored this sweet irony.

As for Mary Magdalene, she was becoming a thorn in his side. Her writings were gaining popularity, reaching more and more people. Her angelic protector was a formidable opponent, keeping his minions at bay. But he was not one to give up so easily. He would find a way to strike, to create doubts in the minds of the believers. His ghouls and goblins, spread across the lands, were stirring up trouble, planting seeds of discord among the faithful. They were whispering in the ears of the religious leaders, questioning the teachings of the apostles, sowing seeds of doubt in their hearts. The Devil knew this was a long game. Patience was key. The apostles, filled with the Holy Spirit, were formidable opponents. But they were still human, prone to despair, doubt, and fear. He would use these weaknesses against them, drive wedges between them and their flock.

The enduring love of Mary Magdalene, the penultimate chapter in the grand saga, bore witness to the enduring love of a redeemed soul. Her transformation from a life of darkness and despair to a life touched by the grace of Jesus was a testament to the limitless power of divine love. As Mary poured her heart into her writings, the Devil seethed with fury at the prospect of her redemption. He sought to poison her thoughts with doubts, tempting her to turn away from her newfound purpose and embrace the shadows of her past. But the angelic forces encircled Mary, their celestial wings shielding her from the Devil's wicked influence. They whispered words of encouragement, reminding her of the unbreakable bond she shared with Jesus. The Devil's voice echoed through the spiritual realm, a snarl dripping with hatred. "Mary, you were meant for darkness, not light. Embrace your sins, revel in your past. Do not let the love of Jesus imprison you." But the angel's voice resonated with unwavering love. "Mary, you are a vessel of divine grace, chosen by Jesus Himself. Your past does not define you; your redemption does. Embrace the love that has set you free and share it with the world." Mary, with tears streaming down her face, continued to write, her words filled with the depth of her love for Jesus and the profound impact He had on her life. Through her testament, she revealed the transformative power of forgiveness, offering hope to all who would read her words.

The journeys of the apostles, carried out in the name of spreading Christ's teachings, were as much personal as they were spiritual. I, Mary Magdalene, a silent witness to these events, understood that the apostles were walking a path paved by prophecies, facing their own realities, and navigating the challenges inherent to their mission.

In Damascus, Thomas faced a barrage of doubt and hostility from locals and travelers alike. "Doubting Thomas," he was often called, a moniker reminding him of his initial skepticism after Christ's resurrection. However, the Holy Spirit fueled him with resilience, and he turned his personal struggle into a tool of connection, allowing others to openly express their doubts and fears. The prophecies of Daniel regarding trials and tribulations rang in his ears, providing a blueprint of endurance.

Elsewhere, Simon the Zealot, known for his fiery temperament, was learning patience. His journey through the Roman Empire's bustling cities was an exercise in restraint and humility. He discovered that the softness of a comforting word often achieved more than the heat of a thousand speeches. The apostles' journeys were filled with challenges and triumphs, each step molding them further into vessels of Christ's love. The Holy Spirit was working through them, turning prophecies into realities, and transforming hearts and souls. In the quiet night, as I pondered over the unfolding narratives, I realized that these weren't just the stories of the apostles, but stories of humanity touched by divine grace. The lines of prophecies were coming alive, painting a picture of redemption, hope, and the promise of God's kingdom on Earth.

The Web of Deceit Through the Devil's Eyes. In the hidden corridors of the world, a malevolent force was gathering strength. Watching, waiting, scheming. From his shadowy throne, the Devil orchestrated a symphony of chaos and despair. The apostles, each on their own path, were facing trials and tribulations, and he was ready to exploit every moment of weakness.

The apostle Thomas found himself in the far reaches of India, where the people revered countless gods and goddesses. Their belief systems were deeply rooted and complex, and Thomas struggled to make them see the path of the one true God. The Devil reveled in the apostle's frustrations and failures; his attempts to convey the Gospel often met with disinterest or outright hostility.

And then there was Philip, journeying to the heart of Scathia, spreading the teachings of Christ to tribes and kingdoms untouched by Roman influence. The Devil observed, intrigued. These were strong, resilient people with their own spiritual beliefs. Philip's mission was not an easy one. He was a stranger, a foreigner, and his words were often met with suspicion and mistrust. But Philip persisted, guided by the Holy Spirit. The Devil watched, silently rooting for his failure.

Meanwhile, the Devil's minions were hard at work, whispering doubts into the ears of the masses, sowing discord among the faithful, stoking the fires of fear and hatred. Each apostle faced their own trials, but it was Mary Magdalene who vexed the Devil the most. Her writings were spreading far and wide, her words bringing comfort and hope to many. He had tried to approach her, to disrupt her mission, but the angel that protected her was relentless. The Devil realized he had to adjust his strategy. Direct attacks weren't working; he needed to be subtler, to undermine the apostles' missions in more insidious ways. So, he began to manipulate the political and religious leaders of the time, using their egos and ambitions as weapons against the spread of the Gospel. As his plans unfolded, the Devil could only wait, biding his time, and revel in the chaos that was beginning to take hold. The apostles had started their mission under the Holy Spirit's guidance, and the divine was working wonders through them. The physical reality reflected the spiritual change, signs and miracles following them as promised in the prophecy of Joel: "I will pour out my Spirit on all people. Your sons and daughters will prophesy, your old men will dream dreams, your young men will see visions."

However, in the spiritual realm, the shadows were beginning to stir. The adversary, the mirror image of God borne from his shadow but oblivious to his origin, watched these events unfold. He was the embodiment of rebellion, the genesis of the seven cardinal sins, an entity consumed by rage and jealousy. Aware of the change in the spiritual climate, he saw the apostles spreading the gospel of Christ. Seeing this shift as a threat, he felt his authority and dominance being challenged. He saw the divine light spreading in places once enveloped in his darkness, and he felt a surge of anger and fear. He was no stranger to prophecies. He knew the Old Testament and the forewarnings of the prophets. However, unlike the apostles, who saw the prophecies as promises and guiding beacons, he saw them as threats and ultimatums. The prophecy of Genesis, where God said to the serpent, "He will crush your head, and you will strike his heel," reverberated in his mind. This prophecy he saw as his downfall, a prophecy that foretold his defeat.

And so, as the apostles continued their divine work, the adversary started to devise his counter-strategy. He rallied his forces and prepared for the spiritual warfare that was about to unfold. He was determined to fight against the prophecy and prevent the fulfillment of God's plan. The shadows stirred. The battle was beginning to take shape. The celestial struggle between good and evil, the war between divine love and diabolical rebellion, was on the horizon. The world was unaware of the storm brewing in the spiritual realm, but it would soon feel its tremors. The echoes of the prophets' words hung heavy in the spiritual atmosphere. The apostles, driven by the Holy Spirit, and the adversary, consumed by pride and wrath, were both ready for their respective missions. The world was their battlefield, and the souls of humankind were their prize.

In the ethereal realm, where elements of reality and metaphysical entities coexisted, the stage was set for a grand contest. The embodiment of the Holy Spirit and the Adversary, manifestations of divine benevolence and malevolent mischief respectively, stood as opposites. The Holy Spirit, embodying the wisdom and teachings of Jesus and the Buddha, sought to spread a message of salvation, integrity, ethical living, and joyous existence. The Demonic Adversary, equipped with the power of the Seven Cardinal Sins, countered with deception, aiming to keep humanity in the clutches of spiritual ignorance and suffering.

This dialogue, laden with philosophical depth and metaphysical intricacies, was not meant for mortal ears. Still, its effects rippled across the fabric of existence, shaping the destiny of individuals and societies alike. The stakes were high, the outcomes were uncertain, and the actors were entities beyond human comprehension.

The Holy Spirit, an entity of warmth and light, initiated the dialogue. "Throughout human history," it began, its voice echoing with the wisdom of sages and saints, "we have witnessed the struggle of individuals striving to lead upright lives, seeking happiness, fulfillment, and spiritual enlightenment. They yearn for salvation, for an escape from the suffering and injustices that riddle their existence." The Holy Spirit further elaborated, "The teachings of Jesus, as well as those of the Buddha, offer a path to such a life. They encourage love, compassion, righteousness, and selfless action. They speak of a state of being where joy, peace, and happiness are not merely fleeting experiences, but a lasting condition of the soul. This is the divine gift of salvation and alignment of the individual will with the Divine Will."

The Adversary, a figure as compelling as it was menacing, responded, its voice laced with cynicism and arrogance. "Your path is demanding," it countered. "It requires individuals to resist the allure of their deepest desires, to face their fears, to constantly strive for an ideal they may never attain. My path offers them immediate satisfaction, a sense of power, and the freedom to fulfill their desires without fear of judgment or retribution."

The Holy Spirit listened, acknowledging the Adversary's perspective. "True, the path is not easy," it conceded. "But it offers something far more profound and enduring than transient pleasures or illusory power. It offers inner peace, unconditional love, and a sense of fulfillment that does not depend on external circumstances."

The debate raged on in the unseen realm, influencing the choices and destinies of countless souls in the physical world. The Holy Spirit, representing the universal principles of love, integrity, and ethical living, clashed with the Adversary's army of doubts, fears, and deceptions, making it a battle of cosmic significance, a battle for the soul of humanity. The setting of this spiritual duel was beyond the dimensions of time and space. Yet its effects could be felt in the hearts and minds of people, guiding their actions and shaping their destinies. This celestial dialogue of salvation and temptation, of righteousness and deceit, continued to unfold, echoing through the realms of existence.

However, despite the colossal struggle, the tone was not one of despair or hopelessness. The Holy Spirit radiated an aura of calm assurance, reminding every soul that the potential for divine grace and salvation resided within them. The power to choose the path of righteousness was theirs, a beacon of hope in the face of adversity, a testament to the resilience of the human spirit in its quest for spiritual enlightenment.

In Rome, Paul had arrived to spread the Word in the heart of the Empire. The Devil turned the Romans' pride against them, using their sense of superiority and their disdain for foreign religions to breed hostility towards Paul and his followers. He filled the minds of the Roman officials with suspicions and stoked their fears, igniting a violent opposition to the Christian faith. Among the Apostles, only Mary Magdalene remained impervious to his attempts to undermine their faith. Every attempt to break her resolve only strengthened her commitment to the cause. Watching her, the Devil was filled with a cold, malignant fury. The more he tried to break her, the stronger she seemed to become. As the Apostles persisted in their mission, facing hardships and persecution, the Devil grew more determined to thwart them. Despite their strength and resilience, he remained confident that he could sow enough discord and despair to silence their voices.

Chapter 5
Perseverance in Persecution

Persecution was an inevitability that the apostles understood from the beginning. Christ had forewarned them, "If they persecuted me, they will persecute you also." And so, they braced themselves for the trials that would test their resolve. The apostles faced scorn and rejection, betrayal by friends, and violence from those who feared the change they represented. They were expelled from synagogues, driven out of towns, and sometimes physically attacked.

The apostle James, for instance, found himself in prison, bound in chains, facing the wrath of King Herod himself. Yet through it all, their faith did not falter. The words of the prophet Jeremiah echoed in their hearts, "But the Lord is with me like a mighty warrior so my persecutors will stumble and not prevail." Simultaneously, the apostles were armed with the knowledge that they were not alone. The Holy Spirit was their constant companion, providing comfort and guidance in their darkest hours. They remembered the words from the prophecy of Isaiah, "When you pass through the waters, I will be with you and when you pass through the rivers, they will not sweep over you."

Mary Magdalene, carrying on her work in the background, documented the apostles' trials and victories. Through her writings, the apostles' teachings continued to spread, inspiring others and giving strength to those facing their own persecutions. This chapter of their lives was a testament to their unwavering faith and perseverance. Their trials only served to solidify their resolve and deepen their commitment to spreading the Gospel. They understood, as conveyed by the Prophet Daniel, that "the people who know their God shall be strong, and carry out great exploits."

As this invisible dialogue raged, it became manifest in the choices individuals made, in the echoes of their words and deeds. The Holy Spirit inspired acts of love, compassion, and mercy, turning hearts to the divine and strengthening their faith. The Adversary's whispers led some down the path of temptation, sowing confusion and fostering discontent. In the bustling marketplaces, people debated the apostles' words, and the promises of salvation they brought. Some, their hearts touched by the Holy Spirit, chose to open themselves to this newfound faith, inspired by the transformative power of divine love. Others, swayed by the Adversary, clung to their old ways, mired in skepticism and doubt, allowing their fears of the unknown to override the truth they glimpsed.

In palaces of power, leaders grappled with the implications of this new faith that was sweeping across their domains. Some chose to embrace it, recognizing the divine wisdom in the teachings of Jesus. They saw how these principles of love, forgiveness, and selflessness could bring about harmony and peace in their lands. Yet, others, under the Adversary's influence, felt threatened by the seismic shift this new faith could bring. They feared losing their grip on power and did everything they could to quash this burgeoning movement, using manipulation and deceit to sow discord.

The Devil's ghouls kept a close eye on Mary, reporting her every move back to him. He learned of her writings and the wisdom they held, detailing the experiences and teachings of Jesus. He saw the threat they posed; these scriptures were another method to disseminate the teachings of Jesus, and he couldn't allow that. He had to interfere. But the Devil was met with an unexpected challenge. Mary was protected. An angel, radiating with divine light, stood guard over her, deflecting his malevolent attempts to interfere with her mission. His attempts to approach her were thwarted, his influence repelled by the heavenly guardian. His resentment towards Mary, the Apostles, and the protective angels grew with each failed attempt.

The Trials and Triumphs:

In their travels, the apostles found strength in unity, drawing on Jesus's teachings, "For where two or three gather in my name, there am I with them." Each apostle, despite the vast distance that separated them, felt this powerful connection. As they met with other believers, shared meals, prayed together, and worshiped, the Holy Spirit moved amongst them, binding them in their common purpose.

Many instances of the Holy Spirit's presence were recorded, its divine influence seen in the miraculous healings, the courage of the apostles, and the love that underpinned their community. A profound moment occurred when Peter healed a lame beggar in the name of Jesus Christ. As the man leapt to his feet, a crowd gathered. The sight of the joyous man jumping and praising God led to many conversions that day. It was as though the Holy Spirit flowed between them, manifesting the love of God and the teachings of Jesus into tangible action. In another instance, when the apostle Thomas was met with disbelief in a distant land, he implored his doubters to gather and pray with him. As they did, a woman who had been blind from birth regained her sight, and the crowd, touched by the Holy Spirit, were left in awe, their doubts extinguished.

And so, it was not an easy path, yet it was one illuminated by triumphs borne from their steadfast faith. Each trial was met head-on, and every victory was a testament to the power of Jesus's teachings and the guidance of the Holy Spirit. The unity and faith of the followers became a beacon for others, further spreading the word of God and attracting more to the fold.

Despite the immense challenges that the apostles and early Christians faced, their perseverance never waned. They were guided by the words of the prophet Isaiah: "But those who hope in the Lord will renew their strength. They will soar on wings like eagles, they will run and not grow weary, they will walk and not be faint."

Chapter 6

Spreading Doubt and Discord Through the Devil's Eyes

A sinister smile stretched across the Devil's countenance as he watched the growing unrest among the followers of Jesus' teachings. The whispers of his goblins and ghouls, infecting their minds with doubt, were beginning to take root. As he observed the Apostles, steadfast in their mission despite the growing hostility, he couldn't help but marvel at their tenacity. Yet, he was not concerned. After all, he was the master of deceit, the weaver of lies. Doubt, the Devil knew, was a potent weapon. It ate away at the foundations of faith, corroded bonds of trust, and bred discontent. And once it took root, it spread like wildfire.

He watched with glee as his minions sowed seeds of skepticism and discord among the communities. Their whispered lies and half-truths were insidious, slowly chipping away at the faith of many. Among his most valuable pawns were the religious leaders who wielded considerable influence over their followers. Their pride and greed made them susceptible to his manipulation. His minions whispered into their ears, fueling their egos, feeding their ambition, and they played right into his hands. They began to speak out against the Apostles, inciting their congregations to reject their teachings. Likewise, politicians were swayed by his influence, using their authority to restrict the Apostles' efforts to spread the Gospel. They used their influence to silence those who dared to speak about Jesus' teachings, adding another layer of difficulty for the Apostles.

Despite the growing opposition, the Apostles continued their mission, bolstered by the Holy Spirit. Their unyielding faith was a constant thorn in the Devil's side, a shining beacon that refused to be snuffed out. But the Devil was not deterred. The battle was far from over. He would use every weapon in his arsenal, exploit every weakness, and stop at nothing to thwart the spread of Jesus' message. As he looked upon the world from his throne of shadows, the Devil plotted his next move. The game was on, and he was eager to play

As the apostles journeyed across the land, spreading the word of Christ and performing miraculous deeds through the power of the Holy Spirit, a looming shadow started to make its presence felt. This shadow was the mirror image of God, a remnant of the original sin that had disconnected mankind from the spiritual realm. This entity despised humanity and was enraged by the newfound connection between God and humans through the Holy Spirit.

The apostles could feel the force of this resentment. It manifested as trials and tribulations, as false prophets sowing doubt among the believers, as persecutions, and sometimes even in the form of nature itself when storms and hardships seemed to hinder their mission. Peter, while in Rome, found himself facing a pretender who claimed to perform miracles through the power of God. However, Peter sensed the shadow in him, the perversions of the man's spirit. Engaging with him in a public confrontation, Peter invoked the power of the Holy Spirit, revealing the truth to the people. The impostor was revealed as a mere man of deceit, his so-called miracles nothing more than illusions. The people, witnessing the power of the true God, reaffirmed their faith.

In another part of the world, Bartholomew faced fierce storms that threatened to capsize his ship. The crew, succumbing to fear, considered this a bad omen. But Bartholomew, steadfast in his faith, prayed, invoking the name of Jesus and the protection of the Holy Spirit. As he did, the storm receded, and they were granted safe passage. His faith inspired his fellow travelers, leading to conversions even amidst the crisis. Each apostle, in their own time and place, had to confront this shadow. And each time, their faith in God and the support of the Holy Spirit proved to be their guiding light, driving away the darkness and affirming the power of the divine.

The Devil observed Mary Magdalene with an amalgam of curiosity and resentment. The woman was a conundrum, an enigma that both intrigued and infuriated him. She had been at Jesus' side through his trials, had witnessed the glory of His resurrection, and was now one of the key supporters of His Apostles. Despite his previous attempts to lure her into his influence, she had remained resolute, her faith a bastion against his persuasive whispers. But the Devil was not one to back down easily. He was the harbinger of chaos, the king of the underworld, and he was determined to disrupt Mary Magdalene's plans.

He seethed at their audacity to disrupt his reign, to spread hope and salvation when he had worked so hard to cultivate despair and corruption. However, frustration did not deter him; instead, it fueled him. The devil knew that where direct intervention failed, subtlety might succeed. He resolved to be more cunning in his approach, manipulating those around Mary to create discord. His ghouls, ready to do his bidding, set forth on their new mission. The Devil watched as they slithered into the hearts and minds of those susceptible to his influence, sowing seeds of suspicion, inciting paranoia, and stoking the fires of fear and anger. The battle between salvation and corruption raged on, and the Devil was intent on ensuring that his malevolence would prevail.

The efforts of the apostles bore fruit as the teachings of Jesus spread across the continents. Word of their miraculous deeds and the power of the Holy Spirit traveled faster than the apostles themselves could, inspiring faith even in places they had yet to reach. In the bustling city of Corinth, the Apostle Paul preached to the Greeks about the teachings of Jesus. Using the wisdom of the Greeks themselves, he showed them how the teachings of Christ fulfilled their philosophical pursuits of truth, beauty, and goodness. His words resonated deeply with the people, leading many to convert to Christianity.

In distant India, Thomas found an eager audience among the spiritually inclined natives. He talked to them of Jesus' teachings, drawing parallels between the principles of compassion, love, and sacrifice found in their own faiths. The people, recognizing the universality of these values, accepted Jesus as a great spiritual teacher, and many chose to follow his teachings. Even in the face of severe persecution in Jerusalem, James stood firm, spreading the word of God with conviction and love. He reminded the Jews of the prophecies, and how Jesus had fulfilled them. Despite facing hostility and threats, his bravery and unwavering faith led many Jews to reconsider their initial skepticism, leading to a growing Christian community within Jerusalem itself.

The apostles, driven by their commitment to Jesus' teachings and empowered by the Holy Spirit, successfully sowed the seeds of Christianity far and wide. Their efforts, often met with hardships and trials, were beginning to transform the spiritual landscape of the world. The apostles would often come together, seeking solace in each other's company. In these gatherings, the Holy Spirit would flow strongly, reaffirming their faith and strengthening their resolve to continue their mission.

From the summit of Mount Ararat, where Noah's ark had once come to rest, the Devil observed the Apostles. His serpentine eyes traced their paths, crisscrossing like spider threads across the vast tapestry of the earth. Each was on a mission to spread the message of Jesus, and each was a thorn in his side. Peter, in Rome, was turning the heart of the empire. John was baptizing in Ephesus, where the Temple of Artemis stood. Andrew was heading east, while his brother, Simon Peter, journeyed west. Each Apostle carried with him the seed of faith, sowing it among the populace, stirring hearts, and awakening minds to the teachings of Jesus.

The Devil looked upon their works with simmering fury. He had been the Lightbringer, the Morning Star, and yet he had been cast out, reduced to a shadow whispering in the wind. He watched as they healed the sick, gave hope to the desperate, and brought together communities. The world was changing, and he did not like it. He sent forth his minions, the ghouls, to each of the Apostles. They would be the whispers of doubt in the crowds, the naysayers in the markets, the inciters of fear in the alleyways. He could not touch the Apostles directly, the protection of the Holy Spirit was too strong, but he could influence those around them. He could create a world where their message fell on deaf ears, where hearts were too hardened by fear and suspicion to accept the message of hope and salvation. His ghouls had their tasks. They whispered into the ears of the powerful, played upon their insecurities and fears, inflamed their lust for power. They spun their tales among the common folk, sowing seeds of doubt and suspicion.

The Apostles were agents of change, and change was frightening. It was a simple matter to fan the flames of fear and turn it into a raging inferno. As the Apostles journeyed on, the Devil watched, a malevolent shadow ever present, ever watching, ever scheming. The war for souls had begun, and he was intent on tipping the scales in his favor.

As word spread and the number of believers grew, so too did the resistance against them. The apostles found themselves facing trials and tribulations from those who felt threatened by the rise of this new faith. In Jerusalem, James was met with growing hostility from the Jewish leaders. They saw the new faith as a heretical sect that was pulling Jews away from their traditional beliefs. James was often called to defend his faith before the Sanhedrin, presenting compelling arguments and demonstrating an unwavering devotion that both infuriated and fascinated his opponents.

Meanwhile, in Rome, Peter faced trials of a different nature. The Roman Empire, known for its religious tolerance, had taken a harsh stance against the followers of Jesus, seeing them as a potential threat to the empire's stability. Peter, despite facing constant threats and bouts of imprisonment, remained steadfast in his mission, drawing strength from the Holy Spirit. Thomas, too, faced numerous trials in India. The caste system in place resisted his message of universal love and equality, causing him to be persecuted by those in power. Yet, he persisted, drawing strength from his faith and the unity he felt when communing with his fellow apostles in spirit. Their trials were many, their path strewn with obstacles. Yet, they persevered, driven by their faith and the power of the Holy Spirit. Every trial served only to reinforce their resolve, proving to them that their mission was far from over. Their struggles only served to highlight the strength of their faith, and with every challenge they overcame, the faith of their followers deepened, and their numbers grew.

In the shadowy depths of Gehenna, the Devil hatched his plans. His cunning knew no bounds, his malice, no limits. The Apostles were spreading the message of salvation far and wide, challenging his authority, threatening his dominion. He would not let them continue unchallenged. Around the obsidian council table, his minions reported the latest news. In Rome, Peter had made inroads with the citizens, gaining followers daily. In Ephesus, John's teachings were resonating with the Greeks. Andrew was bringing the Word of God to Scythians, and Simon Peter was touching hearts in the West. Each update was like a fresh wound, a reminder of his exile from Heaven and a testament to the growing influence of these mortal men.

In his dark heart, resentment bloomed into fury. He had once been the most radiant among the angels, the Morning Star. Yet he had been cast out, banished from the Divine presence, while these mortals were now basking in God's favor. Using his ghouls as extensions of his will, he fanned the flames of resistance. He whispered in the ears of influential senators in Rome, stirring fear and prejudice. He stoked the pride of the priests of Artemis in Ephesus, seeding paranoia about the new faith encroaching upon their territory. To the Scythians, he portrayed Andrew as a foreign invader, trying to uproot their traditions. And in the West, he kindled fear among the powerful, convincing them that Simon Peter's message would destabilize their rule. Yet despite his manipulations, the Apostles' message of love, hope, and salvation spread. Frustration gnawed at the Devil. He saw in the Apostles' work a reflection of the Divine love he had once been a part of. But his pride forbade him from acknowledging his longing, and he subsumed it with fresh waves of anger and resentment. Even so, the Devil watched, waited, and schemed. He understood that the battle would not be won in a single grand gesture but in a thousand small corruptions. So, he cast his net wide, preparing to engulf the world in his shadow.

In these difficult times, the power of faith became the apostles' shield and strength. It sustained them through persecutions, gave them courage to speak truth to power, and propelled them to continue spreading the Gospel. The believers, too, drew strength from their faith, seeing in the apostles the living embodiment of Jesus's teachings and the power of the Holy Spirit. In Jerusalem, James's faith gave him the wisdom and eloquence to refute the accusations of heresy leveled against him. The more he was attacked, the more steadfast he became, his faith unwavering like a rock against the relentless waves. His sermons, filled with love and truth, won over many hearts, even amongst those who initially stood against him.

In Rome, Peter's faith was his refuge in the face of constant threats and imprisonment. It gave him the strength to endure, to continue preaching Jesus's message of love and salvation, even as the mighty Roman Empire sought to quell the rise of Christianity. His faith became an inspiration to the believers in Rome, a beacon of light in the darkest of times. In India, Thomas's faith became a testament to the power of love and equality. Despite the persecution, he continued to preach Jesus's message, his words resonating deeply within the hearts of many who felt oppressed by the caste system. His faith became a symbol of hope, inspiring a surge of new believers. In each corner of the world, the apostles, guided by the Holy Spirit, made tremendous strides in spreading the Gospel. Their faith, unyielding in the face of adversity, became a testament to the transformative power of Jesus's teachings and the Holy Spirit. And it was this faith, the unwavering belief in the promise of salvation, that continued to draw more and more believers into the fold.

Bitterness and resentment were his constant companions as the Devil observed the ever-expanding reach of the Apostles' message. The Apostle Thomas had taken the teachings of Jesus to India, a land rife with ancient and diverse philosophies. How dare these humble Apostles bring new words to lands so steeped in tradition and knowledge? A flame of fury sparked within the Devil at this audacity. He looked upon the distant subcontinent and saw opportunities to weave his own dark tapestry. The ghouls and goblins, his loyal minions, sprang into action, spreading whispered rumors and false miracles to undermine the work of Thomas. He fueled the skepticism of the people, reminding them of their own spiritual traditions, casting the Apostle as a trespasser. Yet, as much as the Devil despised the Apostles, Mary Magdalene was an enigma that he found increasingly fascinating and infuriating. This woman who had been so close to Jesus, who now held a role of leadership among his followers, was seemingly untouchable, protected by an angel of radiant power. He dared to approach her, attempting to cast doubt in her mind, to make her question her faith and her mission. But she was resolute, unfazed by his insinuations. He remembered how he'd once stood in the presence of the Divine, resolute in his own beliefs, only to be cast out. The memory fueled his resentment. In spite of his efforts, Mary remained a steadfast beacon of faith, and the Apostles continued their work unswerving. This did not deter the Devil. He reminded himself that patience was the key. He would bide his time, let the seeds of mistrust and discord he'd planted take root and grow. He knew how to exploit human weaknesses, their fear, and their pride. It was only a matter of time.

As the apostles carried on their holy mission, the numbers of believers grew exponentially. Their teachings spread like ripples in a pond, each believer influencing others and inspiring new followers. However, with this growth also came a significant increase in opposition. In Jerusalem, the Pharisees and Sadducees were distressed by the rising influence of the apostles. Fearful of the threat to their power, they plotted to undermine the apostles' teachings and discredit them among the people. They set traps for James in public debates, hoping to trip him up and expose him as a false prophet. In Rome, the ruling elites viewed the growing Christian community with suspicion. The teachings of equality and love for all were a stark contrast to the prevailing hierarchy. Peter found himself being investigated by the Roman authorities, who perceived his message as a challenge to their authority. In India, the local priests felt threatened by Thomas's message of love and equality, which contradicted the rigid caste system. They rallied against him, declaring his teachings heretical and stirring up the local populace against the Christian converts. But each time, the apostles, guided by the Holy Spirit, responded with wisdom and humility. James used the Pharisees' own scriptures to counter their arguments, winning the respect of many. Peter, while imprisoned, converted his jailer, who in turn spread the message of Jesus among the Roman guards. In India, Thomas performed miracles of healing, leading even the skeptics to question their opposition. As the opposition grew, so did the apostles' resolve, reinforcing their commitment to their holy mission.

Chapter 7

Shadows of Fear Through the Devil's Eyes

The Devil, shrouded in the comfort of darkness, watched as Philip carried the word of God to the Hellenistic cities. He had always found the Greeks fascinating. Their minds were different, full of questioning spirits and boundless curiosity. They cherished wisdom and the art of argument, traits the devil admired, traits he could exploit. Through the whispers of the shadows, he sowed the seeds of philosophical conflict. The ghouls and goblins carried rumors that toyed with the Greeks' insatiable hunger for debate. Could this new God withstand the rigorous examination of the Greeks? Or would they dismiss him as just another tale in their pantheon of myths?

Yet, the devil noticed something else. The Greeks were drawn to the message of love and unity carried by Philip. Many had grown tired of the capricious gods and their constant bickering, intrigued by the concept of a single, loving deity. This was a setback, a threat to the devil's influence, but he was not discouraged. Every light casts a shadow, and in those shadows, the devil thrived. His attention then shifted back to Mary Magdalene. He despised her unwavering faith, her strength, her complete devotion. Yet, despite himself, he couldn't help but acknowledge her commitment. How could someone so simple, so human, be so resilient? The devil's resentment grew, stoked by the flames of his pride and anger.

As the apostles' influence spread, the devil realized his attempts to undermine their mission had only pushed them to work harder. His approach had to change. He needed a more subtle plan, a method of striking at the heart of the followers of Jesus. Thus, he decided to target the unity that was the source of their strength. If he could fracture that, he could start to destabilize the fledgling faith.

In every city the apostles traveled, miracles accompanied their words and deeds, reinforcing the divine truth of their message. The miracles manifested in different ways: some were healed, some were delivered from evil spirits, while others experienced radical transformations in their lives. In Antioch, John was able to heal a young boy who had been struck dumb since birth. Word spread quickly of this miracle, attracting crowds from neighboring towns. More than just a demonstration of divine power, this miracle was also a testament to the love and compassion that lay at the core of Jesus' teachings.

In Athens, Paul found himself among a group of Greek philosophers who were skeptical of his teachings. Challenged to prove his claims, Paul healed a man who had been crippled from birth right in front of their eyes. This miracle softened their skepticism and opened their minds to his message.

In Alexandria, Philip found a possessed man, tormented by an evil spirit. In a dramatic encounter, Philip commanded the spirit to leave the man in the name of Jesus. The spirit was expelled, and the man was freed from his torment. News of this event spread rapidly, causing many in the city to seek out Philip's teachings. Each of these miracles served as a testament to the divine authority behind the apostles' mission. But beyond that, they also illustrated the transformational power of their message. The healed boy in Antioch could now speak of God's love, the once-crippled man in Athens could walk in God's path, and the freed man in Alexandria could live his life unburdened. These miracles not only expanded the apostles' influence but also served as powerful testaments to the living truth of Jesus' teachings, inspiring many to embrace His message of love and redemption.

The Devil observed the apostle Philip as he joined forces with Andrew, who was called to spread the Word of Jesus towards the East. They had come far, spreading the message of God to the people of Scythia, and the devil was intrigued by their determination. Andrew had a daunting task. From the desolate steppe of Mongolia to the heart of China, a land rich in ancient wisdom, he had to travel. Philip, on the other hand, stayed behind in Scythia, working diligently to plant the seeds of faith among the people. The devil watched from his dark corner as Andrew parted ways with Philip, venturing into the unforgiving landscape, climbing over towering mountains, passing through desolate plains, and rocky terrains. His resolve was admirable, his spirit undying. It stirred a sick sense of curiosity within the devil, a perverse desire to test the apostle's spirit. Using his power, the devil conjured up a brutal storm. The snow whipped violently against Andrew, but he trudged forward, his faith acting as a beacon, guiding him through the blinding blizzard. His determination was strong, but the devil knew that physical strength could waver. Next, the devil turned his attention to the warlords, manipulating their greed and fear. He whispered into the ears of the most powerful among them, playing on their superstitions, and painting Andrew as a threat to their power. He was pleased to see his plans coming to fruition when the warlords dispatched their soldiers to hunt down Andrew.

As the apostles continued their divine mission, their journey was not without hardships. They faced trials of different kinds, often from those who did not understand or accept their teachings. Persecution, ridicule, and threats were part of their daily experiences. But despite these challenges, their resolve remained unbroken, their faith unwavering. In Jerusalem, Peter and John were arrested by temple guards for preaching about Jesus in the Temple grounds. They were brought before the Sanhedrin, the Jewish ruling council, where they were sternly warned not to speak or teach in the name of Jesus. Undeterred, Peter spoke eloquently of their mission and the transformative power of Jesus' teachings. Astonished by Peter and John's courage, the council released them with a stern warning. This event only strengthened their determination to continue spreading the Gospel.

In Ephesus, Thomas faced opposition from the silversmiths whose livelihood depended on the worship of the goddess Artemis. His preaching was turning many away from their idols, threatening their business. A violent mob formed, forcing Thomas to flee for his life. Still, he remained undeterred, using this experience to reflect on the allure of false idols and the importance of unwavering faith.

While the apostles' mission brought them face to face with these trials, they also found an inner strength born from their deep faith and their firsthand experiences with Jesus. They stood strong amidst challenges, often turning these trials into opportunities for deeper understanding and growth. Their perseverance bore witness to the transformative power of their faith and served as an inspiring testament to those who heard their teachings. They reminded their followers that trials and tribulations were often part of one's spiritual journey, but with faith, one could overcome and emerge stronger

The teachings of the apostles brought about a significant change in the hearts and minds of the people. As they continued to spread the gospel, stories of miracles, healings, and conversions became more common, sparking a religious awakening across different regions. In Samaria, Philip was known for his healing miracles, casting out unclean spirits, and even raising the dead. His ministry was a beacon of hope to those in pain, and it led to an influx of new believers in Jesus' teachings. He spent much of his time

Chapter 8

The Final Days of the Apostles

The Apostle's journey was not endless, and as the years passed, they faced their final days on earth, bearing the cost of their tireless work. Yet, their faith and the strength of the Holy Spirit never faltered. They continued spreading Jesus's teachings until their last breath, knowing well the impact their actions would have on future generations.

In Jerusalem, James met his end with grace and conviction. He was arrested by Jewish authorities and sentenced to death for his unwavering commitment to spreading the Gospel. James's courage in the face of death inspired many, cementing his place as one of the most respected figures in Christian history. In Rome, Peter also faced persecution from Roman authorities. His faith remained unshaken, and he continued his ministry, encouraging believers and spreading the Gospel until he was arrested. According to tradition, Peter asked to be crucified upside down, feeling unworthy to die in the same manner as Jesus. His request was granted, turning his death into a powerful symbol of humility and devotion.

Paul's journey ended in Rome, where he was arrested and imprisoned. He spent his final days writing letters to the churches he helped establish, offering words of hope, encouragement, and instruction.

His writings, full of wisdom and spiritual insights, would later form a significant part of the New Testament. Paul was eventually beheaded, his death marking the end of an era.

John, the beloved disciple, lived a long life, outliving the other apostles. He continued his ministry, writing the Book of Revelation and the Gospel of John, contributing further to the Christian canon. His writings, filled with visions, metaphors, and profound spiritual insights, added depth to the understanding of Jesus's teachings. According to tradition, John died of old age in Ephesus, his death marking the end of the Apostolic Age.

Their journeys completed, the apostles left behind a legacy that transformed the world. Their courage, conviction, and relentless dedication to spreading the Gospel were instrumental in the formation and growth of the early Christian Church. Their teachings, preserved in the New Testament, continue to guide Christians worldwide, a testament to their enduring impact. As the apostolic era came to an end, the legacy of the apostles had just begun. The seeds they had sown across the world had taken root, sprouting communities of believers that were growing in number, even in the face of persecution.

In Jerusalem, the teachings of James were kept alive by his followers, providing a strong Christian foundation in the heart of Jewish territory. The city would become a significant location for Christianity, drawing pilgrims from across the world even to this day. In Rome, the memory of Peter's sacrifice inspired generations of believers. It strengthened their resolve, reminding them of the apostle's humility and unwavering faith in the face of adversity. Peter's actions contributed to the city's future as a cornerstone of Christian faith, eventually becoming home to the Papacy.

Paul's letters, circulated among the churches, served as critical instructions for Christian living. His teachings on love, faith, and salvation continue to be central to Christian doctrine. His profound understanding of the Gospel, coupled with his personal experiences, helped shape Christianity as a faith that transcended ethnic and social boundaries.

The long life and writings of John had a lasting impact on Christian theology. The Gospel of John, with its unique perspective on Jesus's life, offered a deeper understanding of Jesus's divinity. His visions, recorded in the Book of Revelation, provided hope and a glimpse into what Christians believe will be the end times.

Their stories, carried through the ages, have inspired countless believers. Their teachings, faithfully recorded and disseminated, became the bedrock of the Christian faith. The apostles, from their humble beginnings to their extraordinary ends, exemplify the transformative power of faith and commitment. Even today, as modern believers gather in worship, the echo of the apostles' words can be heard. When two or more come together in Jesus's name, just as the apostles often did, there's a tangible sense of the Holy Spirit at work, reminding them of their roots and the legacy that they carry forward.

The Enduring Love of Mary Magdalene.

Mary Magdalene, the penultimate chapter in the grand saga, bore witness to the enduring love of a redeemed soul. Her transformation from a life of darkness and despair to a life touched by the grace of Jesus was a testament to the limitless power of divine love. As Mary poured her heart into her writings, the Devil seethed with fury at the prospect of her redemption. He sought to poison her thoughts with doubts, tempting her to turn away from her newfound purpose and embrace the shadows of her past. But the angelic forces encircled Mary, their celestial wings shielding her from the Devil's wicked influence. They whispered words of encouragement, reminding her of the unbreakable bond she shared with Jesus.

The Devil's voice echoed through the spiritual realm, a snarl dripping with hatred. "Mary, you were meant for darkness, not light. Embrace your sins, revel in your past. Do not let the love of Jesus imprison you." But the angel's voice resonated with unwavering love. "Mary, you are a vessel of divine grace, chosen by Jesus Himself. Your past does not define you, your redemption does. Embrace the love that has set you free and share it with the world." Mary, with tears streaming down her face, continued to write, her words filled with the depth of her love for Jesus and the profound impact He had on her life. Through her testament, she revealed the transformative power of forgiveness, offering hope to all who would read her words.

In the annals of our journey, the tale of James, the brother of Jesus, unfolded with both triumphs and tribulations. As I, Mary Magdalene, chronicled his extraordinary path, the angel and the Devil engaged in a heated debate about the religious leaders who sought to thwart James' mission. The angel, ever steadfast in his commitment to the divine plan, urged James to stay strong in the face of opposition. "Do not falter, James," the angel's voice resonated in my mind, echoing the encouragement it offered to James himself. "Your faith is unwavering, and God's truth shall prevail." But the Devil, a cunning adversary, whispered doubts into the hearts of the religious leaders. He sought to manipulate them, sowing seeds of discord and skepticism. His malevolent voice insinuated that James was a mere mortal, unworthy of the authority he claimed. He fueled their jealousy and fear, goading them to take action against James and his followers.

In the Temple courts, James stood resolute, his voice filled with conviction as he preached the Gospel. His words carried the weight of divine truth, challenging the religious leaders' tightly held beliefs. The Devil, seething with anger, unleashed his minions to incite unrest among the people, to turn them against James and his message. The religious leaders, their egos bruised and threatened by James' unwavering faith, conspired to undermine his influence. They questioned his authority, seeking to discredit his divine connection and dissuade the people from following him.

In the depths of the unseen realm, the Devil reveled in the chaos and division he had sown. He mocked James' conviction, relishing in the discord he had created. "He is but a mortal," the Devil sneered, his voice dripping with disdain. "How can he claim to possess divine knowledge? Do not be swayed by his words." The angel, standing firm in his defense of James, countered with words of unwavering faith. "His lineage may be of mortal flesh, but his spirit is guided by the Holy One," the angel proclaimed, his voice steady and resolute. "Do not be deceived by the whispers of darkness. Embrace the light and the truth it reveals." As James faced opposition and endured the trials set before him, his faith burned brighter, his resolve unyielding. The angel's guidance became his source of strength, empowering him to persevere amidst the storm of doubt and hostility.

In the confines of my writing sanctuary, I continued to record these events, penning the trials and triumphs of James' journey. The angel's whispers of hope and the Devil's malicious schemes formed the backdrop of my narrative, an interplay of divine providence and diabolical interference. The chapters flowed seamlessly, the story unfolding with a mystical rhythm. Each page turned, a testament to the unwavering faith of the apostles and the invisible forces that sought to shape their destinies. The tale wove together the perspectives of the angel and the Devil, their conversations mirroring the ongoing struggle for the souls of humankind. As the ink flowed onto the parchment, the clash between light and darkness became more pronounced. The angel's voice, gentle yet resolute, guided James through the tempestuous waters of opposition. The Devil's whispers of doubt and manipulation grew louder, threatening to consume the faith of those who dared to listen. But within the depths of my soul, a spark of hope ignited. The angel's voice reverberated, reminding me that the battles fought on the spiritual plane would ultimately lead to a glorious victory. The apostles were not alone in their struggles; they were supported by celestial forces, guided by divine providence. And so, I continued to write, capturing the timeless tale of faith, resilience, and the eternal clash between good and evil.

The journey of the apostles was far from over, and with each passing chapter, the stakes grew higher, the challenges more formidable. The argument for Jesus' salvation seemed to hold a profound truth that despite our flaws and sins, we are capable of great love and goodness. This inherent capacity to choose good over evil, virtue over sin, was the crux of the salvation promise. This complex tapestry of moral choices and spiritual journeys was woven against the backdrop of bustling marketplaces and grand palaces, places where ordinary and extraordinary lives intersected. It was a historical moment that was not only a testament to the eternal struggle between light and darkness but also a beacon of hope, symbolizing the indomitable human spirit's ability to choose love, joy, and righteousness, even in the face of daunting odds. The saga continued, each apostle's tale intertwining with the celestial dance of angelic guidance and diabolical schemes. With every turn of the page, the struggle between the forces of light and darkness grew more intense, setting the stage for a climactic confrontation that would test the faith and resolve of all involved.

Meanwhile, James found himself battling both skepticism and hostility in Jerusalem. He faced the Sanhedrin, priests, and common folk alike, often witnessing their stubborn resistance to the teachings of Christ. Yet he pressed on, his faith unwavering. Every convert was a victory, a beacon of hope. Yet, the Devil, ever watchful, saw each soul saved as a failure on his part. His frustration grew, his nefarious plans seemed to be continually thwarted. But the Devil was nothing if not persistent, and his plotting against James and the growing Christian community intensified.

As James' journey unfolded in the heart of Jerusalem, he found himself immersed in a battle of epic proportions. His every deed was witnessed. The Sanhedrin, priests, and zealous followers of the established order questioned and debated his every word. They sought to undermine his faith, to discredit the teachings of Christ, and to protect their own power. In the shadowy corners of the Holy City, James engaged in passionate debates with religious authorities. He skillfully defended the ministry of Jesus, presenting irrefutable evidence of the miracles and transformative power that had been witnessed by many. But his opponents, threatened by his message, refused to acknowledge the truth.

As the debates escalated, the religious leaders became increasingly vindictive and sought to silence James. A crowd, driven by anger and hatred, seized him while he was worshiping outside the temple. They staged a mock trial, overseen by the rabbis of the Sanhedrin, and swiftly declared him guilty of heresy. In a frenzied act of insanity, the mob hurled James from the walls of the tabernacle. He crashed onto the stony ground below, broken and bloodied. The crowd, fueled by their anger, began stoning him, their fury unleashed upon the apostle who dared challenge their authority.

Mary was preaching to a congregation, fervently sharing the message of salvation, when she suddenly found herself caught in a vision. Her guardian angel revealed to her the tragic fate that had befallen James. She returned to her physical body, her heart heavy with grief and determination. Without hesitation, Mary sent a message to the senior members of her congregation, urging them to gather and recover

James' body. They needed to act swiftly, guided by the Holy Spirit, to honor their fallen brother and seek guidance for their next steps. With tears streaming down her face, Mary sat at her writing desk, the weight of sorrow bearing down upon her as she chronicled the day's events in her records. She recorded every detail, capturing the tragedy and the unwavering faith of James in the face of persecution.

Clad in a shawl, Mary ventured into the streets of Jerusalem, making her way towards the place where James lay, broken and cold. The city pulsed with tension and uncertainty, as the devil reveled in the chaos and plotted his next move. He sought to make Mary's life unbearable, just as he had done with James.

But Mary, guided and protected by her guardian angel, remained resolute in her faith. She knew that her time in Jerusalem was drawing to a close, for the city would soon face the wrath of the Romans, as her vision had foretold. She had a choice: to make a journey to Ethiopia with a dear sister from her congregation or to embark on a mission to Europe, where the other apostles had spread the gospel. As she walked through the bustling streets of Jerusalem, the aromas of the market mingling with the cries of the souls longing for salvation, Mary experienced a flash of insight. She realized that she needed to complete her records, to gather the stories of Jesus and the apostles, and carry them to the corners of the earth. In her heart, she felt a deep longing to join the apostle who was planning to bring the gospel to Spain and continue spreading the message to France and the British Isles. Though the separation from Mary, the mother of Jesus, was painful, she knew she had family waiting for her in the lands of Kashmir. Mary's thoughts swirled with a mix of sorrow and determination. She knew she couldn't stay in Jerusalem, for the political unrest would soon attract the attention of the Romans. And so, with a heavy heart and the weight of the gospel on her shoulders, she prepared to leave the fertile grounds of salvation that had taken root in the hearts of the people of Jerusalem. Every convert she had brought to the faith was a victory, a testament to the transformative power of Jesus. Though the Devil seethed with frustration at each soul saved, Mary knew her mission was far from over. She would continue to spread the message of salvation, bringing hope to every corner of the earth, even as the trials and tribulations mounted.

The Devil, ever watchful, plotted and schemed, determined to thwart the efforts of the apostles and their growing Christian community. But Mary, fortified by her faith and protected by her guardian angel, stood resolute, ready to face whatever challenges lay ahead.

In the grand cosmic arena, the Devil, acting as the advocate for human fallibility, squared off with the Angel, the advocate for divine redemption. Their ethereal conversation reverberated through the hearts of the individuals on earth, creating an atmosphere of heightened introspection and transformation. The Devil smirked, spinning words like an intricate web, "You see, even Marcus Aurelius, in his wisdom, acknowledged the darker aspects of human nature. He wrote, 'The object of life is not to be on the side of the majority, but to escape finding oneself in the ranks of the insane.' This insanity, the chaos, is borne out of the very sins I speak of." The Angel, representative of the Holy Spirit, responded, its voice serene yet powerful, "Yes, humans may falter, they may succumb to these darker aspects. But Marcus Aurelius also emphasized the human capacity for change, for betterment. He said, 'Waste no more time arguing what a good man should be. Be one.' And that is what Jesus' teachings inspire in people: to be good, to be virtuous." On the earthly plane, echoes of this cosmic dialogue resonated in the minds of the people. They felt the tug of their own darker desires, the seven deadly sins whispering their destructive temptations. Yet, they also felt the call to virtue, to embrace the teachings of Jesus, Buddha, and others.

In the bustling marketplaces, a woman found herself torn between greed and generosity. She was a merchant, and her livelihood depended on the profit she made. Yet, as she heard the apostles speak of Jesus' teachings, of love, and of charity, she felt an overwhelming urge to help those less fortunate. In this moment of introspection, she felt the cosmic dialogue within her, the temptation of greed against the virtue of generosity.

In the grand palaces, a monarch wrestled with his pride and humility. He had always ruled with an iron fist, considering his word as the ultimate law. Yet, the growing popularity of the apostles' message sparked a conflict within him. He remembered the words of Buddha, "Be kind whenever possible. It is always possible." The tension between pride and humility, the struggle of power and kindness, reverberated in his heart.

Everywhere, people faced their own versions of these moral dilemmas, their lives reflecting the cosmic debate between the Devil and the Angel. Yet, amidst these trials, the promise of salvation was a beacon of hope. It reminded people that while they may stumble, they could rise again, stronger and wiser. Many, upon hearing the apostles' words, chose the path of virtue, their hearts touched by the transformative power of divine love. They embraced the teachings of Jesus, embarking on a journey towards self-betterment and communal harmony.

In the end, the message of Jesus resonated, standing as a testament to the human spirit's strength. It echoed the wisdom of Buddha's teachings, Marcus Aurelius's philosophies, and Dalai Lama's guidance, all pointing towards the path of love, compassion, forgiveness, and integrity. Despite the Devil's influence, despite the temptations of the seven deadly sins, people chose the path of virtue, faith, and love. They chose salvation, they chose happiness, and in doing so, they made their stand against the darkness. They proved that the light of the human spirit, fortified by divine guidance, could overcome even the most daunting odds. And thus, the discourse continued, with each person's life serving as a testament to their capacity for virtue and their resilience in the face of temptation. As they navigated their moral landscapes, they proved that even amidst trials and tribulations, the light of faith could illuminate the path towards redemption and salvation.

In thechaotic streets of Jerusalem, Mary Magdalene immersed herself in the sacred task of nurturing the growing flock of Christ. Her days were filled with tending to the women who sought solace and understanding, helping them grasp the profound teachings of Jesus. As the sun set, Mary retreated to her humble abode, where she poured her thoughts onto parchment, transcribing the revelations of the apostles' trials and triumphs as relayed by her guardian angel. In the intimate space of her writing chamber, Mary entered into a deep communion with her guardian angel. Their connection was profound, as they exchanged whispers of divine wisdom and guidance.

Mary's pen danced across the parchment, capturing the essence of the apostles' tribulations, their unwavering faith in the face of persecution, and the miracles they witnessed as the Holy Spirit worked through them. But the Devil, sensing the threat of Mary's influential role in spreading the message of salvation, stirred restlessly in the shadows. He sought to undermine her efforts, knowing that the religious leaders of Jerusalem were susceptible to his corrupt influence. Without the protection of the Holy Spirit, they were easily swayed by his insidious whispers, clouding their hearts with doubt and envy.

As James, the brother of Jesus, had been center stage in the streets of Jerusalem, proclaiming the story of his divine sibling, the Devil had intensified his efforts. He employed cunning strategies to sow discord among the religious leaders, fueling their resentment and fear of the growing influence of the followers of Christ. In the midst of this spiritual battle, Mary's guardian angel delivered the daily trials of the apostles to her. Their stories unfolded like a tapestry of devotion and sacrifice, intertwined with moments of divine intervention.

Mary listened intently, her heart filled with both awe and concern for her beloved disciples. She relayed their experiences with utmost care and precision, ensuring that the words transcribed carried the weight of their unwavering faith. The dialogue between Mary and her guardian angel was a dance of revelation and understanding. She sought guidance on how to navigate the challenges that lay ahead, how to shield her flock from the Devil's deceptions, and how to empower them with the transformative power of God's love.

As this episode of Mary's life draws to a close, Mary's pen halts momentarily, capturing the final words of the apostles' trials for the day. She gazes upon the parchment, a testament to the enduring strength of the followers of Christ. In the depths of her soul, she prepares herself for the next day's revelations, knowing that the battle between light and darkness will continue to unfold. The journey of Mary, both the beloved disciple and Mary, the mother of Jesus, intertwines with the cosmic struggle against evil. Their role in nurturing the faith of the women of Jerusalem becomes an essential thread in the tapestry of salvation. With each passing moment, the stakes grow higher, the challenges more daunting, but Mary's unwavering faith and connection with the divine guide her steps.

Chapter 9
The Healing Touch.

In the vibrant city of Jerusalem, Mary Magdalene continues her ministry among the women, offering solace, guidance, and a listening ear to those burdened by the struggles of life. Her days are filled with a myriad of encounters, each revealing the power of compassion and the transformative touch of God's grace. One day, as Mary walks through the crowded streets, she comes across a woman whose eyes are filled with tears. Sensing her deep anguish, Mary approaches her, extending a gentle hand. The woman shares her story of pain and brokenness, of years spent battling illness and despair. With unwavering empathy, Mary offers a heartfelt prayer, calling upon the healing power of Jesus to bring restoration and wholeness.

In the backdrop of these encounters, the Devil watches intently, recognizing the profound impact of Mary's compassionate acts. He schemes and plots, seeking to exploit the vulnerability of the religious leaders who view her with suspicion and resentment. The Devil whispers into their ears, sowing seeds of doubt and fear, hoping to extinguish the growing flame of faith in the hearts of the people. But Mary's guardian angel, a steadfast companion, encourages her with divine wisdom and strength. Together, they navigate the treacherous waters of opposition and persecution, holding onto the promise of God's love and the transformative power of healing. Each day brings new challenges and triumphs. Mary's hands become instruments of God's mercy, as she witnesses the blind receiving sight, the lame finding strength to walk, and the broken-hearted experiencing profound healing. The stories of these miraculous encounters weave together to form a tapestry of hope and redemption, igniting a spark of faith within the hearts of all who witness them.

As Mary continues her ministry, the religious leaders grow increasingly threatened by the influence she wields. They conspire to undermine her, spreading rumors and false accusations to discredit her mission. But Mary remains steadfast, her resolve fueled by the divine power that flows through her. In the quiet moments of reflection, Mary engages in profound conversations with her guardian angel. They discuss the intricacies of human suffering, the transformative nature of healing, and the constant battle between darkness and light. These conversations provide her with spiritual nourishment, strengthening her resolve to press on despite the mounting opposition.

As the saga continues, Mary's heart is filled with both gratitude and determination. Gratitude for the lives touched by God's healing grace, and determination to continue spreading the message of love and restoration. The Devil's plans may persist, but Mary's unwavering faith, coupled with the divine protection bestowed upon her, serves as a shield against his malevolent schemes.

As the celestial tapestry of human destiny unfurled, Mary found herself at the center of a cosmic battle. In the depths of her soul, she felt the weight of responsibility as she chronicled the apostles' journey through the lens of her unique perspective. Amidst the bustling streets of Jerusalem, Mary's days were filled with aiding and empowering women, helping them understand Jesus' teachings and find their place in a world dominated by patriarchal norms. Her nights were devoted to transcribing the revelations brought by the apostles' guardian angels, who wove a celestial thread of guidance and wisdom into the fabric of their lives.

In the quietude of her chamber, Mary engaged in deep conversations with her guardian angel, exploring the nature of existence and the eternal battle between light and darkness. Together, they contemplated the significance of the apostles' mission, their encounters with advanced celestial technology, and the cosmic forces that shaped their path. As Mary delved deeper into her writings, she discovered that the challenges faced by the apostles were not limited to earthly conflicts. Cosmic beings sought to sway the apostles' resolve, using their own brand of advanced technology and manipulation to test their faith. One such being was Azrael, a powerful celestial entity fascinated by the potential of humanity and determined to shape their destiny. Azrael engaged in philosophical debates with James, challenging his beliefs and exploring the intricacies of free will, destiny, and the role of faith in a universe governed by advanced scientific principles.

Despite the Devil's influence, despite the temptations of the seven deadly sins, people chose the path of virtue, faith, and love. They chose salvation, they chose happiness, and in doing so, they made their stand against the darkness. They proved that the light of the human spirit, fortified by divine guidance, could overcome even the most daunting odds. And thus, the discourse continued, with each person's life serving as a testament to their capacity for virtue and their resilience in the face of temptation. As they navigated their moral landscapes, they proved that even amidst trials and tribulations, the light of faith could illuminate the path towards redemption and salvation.

In the bustling streets of Jerusalem, Mary Magdalene immersed herself in the sacred task of nurturing the growing flock of Christ.

Her days were filled with tending to the women who sought solace and understanding, helping them grasp the profound teachings of Jesus. As the sun set, Mary retreated to her humble abode, where she poured her thoughts onto parchment, transcribing the revelations of the apostles' trials and triumphs as relayed by her guardian angel. In the intimate space of her writing chamber, Mary entered into a deep communion with her guardian angel. Their connection was profound, as they exchanged whispers of divine wisdom and guidance.

Mary's pen danced across the parchment, capturing the essence of the apostles' tribulations, their unwavering faith in the face of persecution, and the miracles they witnessed as the Holy Spirit worked through them. But the Devil, sensing the threat of Mary's influential role in spreading the message of salvation, stirred restlessly in the shadows. He sought to undermine her efforts, knowing that the religious leaders of Jerusalem were susceptible to his corrupt influence. Without the protection of the Holy Spirit, they were easily swayed by his insidious whispers, clouding their hearts with doubt and envy.

As James, the brother of Jesus, had been center stage in the streets of Jerusalem, proclaiming the story of his divine sibling, the Devil had intensified his efforts. He employed cunning strategies to sow discord among the religious leaders, fueling their resentment and fear of the growing influence of the followers of Christ. In the midst of this spiritual battle, Mary's guardian angel delivered the daily trials of the apostles to her. Their stories unfolded like a tapestry of devotion and sacrifice, intertwined with moments of divine intervention. Mary listened intently, her heart filled with both awe and concern for her beloved disciples. She relayed their experiences with utmost care and precision, ensuring that the words transcribed carried the weight of their unwavering faith. The dialogue between Mary and her guardian angel was a dance of revelation and understanding. She sought guidance on how to navigate the challenges that lay ahead, how to shield her flock from the Devil's deceptions, and how to empower them with the transformative power of God's love.

As this episode of Mary's life draws to a close, Mary's pen halts momentarily, capturing the final words of the apostles' trials for the day. She gazes upon the parchment, a testament to the enduring strength of the followers of Christ. In the depths of her soul, she prepares herself for the next day's revelations, knowing that the battle between light and darkness will continue to unfold. The journey of Mary, both the beloved disciple and Mary, the mother of Jesus, intertwines with the cosmic struggle against evil. Their role in nurturing the faith of the women of Jerusalem becomes an essential thread in the tapestry of salvation. With each passing moment, the stakes grow higher, the challenges more daunting, but Mary's unwavering faith and connection with the divine guide her steps.

Chapter 10
Unholy Council

Within the grand council chamber of the ruling monarch, a fierce debate ensued. The Councilmen, men of influence and authority, found themselves embroiled in the philosophical dilemma sparked by the new faith's advent. The Devil saw this as fertile ground to sow seeds of doubt and discord. He whispered in the ears of the skeptical Councilmen, exploiting their fears of losing control, "This new faith, it threatens your rule, your authority. It asks people to turn away from your established order and embrace a power you cannot control." However, some Councilmen had hearts touched by the divine. The wisdom of Jesus' teachings, the transformative power of love, forgiveness, and humility, had resonated with them. One of them, an older and wiser man, took the floor, his words imbued with conviction, "Remember Marcus Aurelius' words: 'The best revenge is not to be like your enemy.' We must not succumb to fear and prejudice." Yet, the Devil persisted, subtly employing the sins of wrath and pride to stoke the fires of resistance, "They challenge your sovereignty. They undermine your authority. Do you not feel the sting of this affront? The audacity of their presumption?" The wise Councilman, though, was not swayed. He remembered the teachings of Buddhist spiritual leaders, "Anger, pride, and jealousy never solve problems, only create more." He appealed to his fellow councilmen, "We must not let fear guide us. Let us understand this new faith, not reject it blindly."

The Angel, embodying the Holy Spirit, echoed through the wise Councilman's voice, "Jesus taught us to 'Love thy neighbor as thyself.' He urged us to seek understanding, forgiveness, and love above all else. Let us embody these virtues in our dealings." With this, the Council was divided. Some felt threatened by the transformative power of this new faith, their decisions influenced by the Devil's temptations. Yet, others were moved by the teachings of Jesus, Marcus Aurelius, and the Dalai Lama, their hearts opened to the possibility of a harmonious co-existence between the new faith and the established order. This division mirrored the cosmic dialogue between the Devil and the Angel. It was a testament to the eternal struggle between faith and doubt, between fear and love, between the seven deadly sins and the seven virtues. In the end, the debate remained unresolved. Yet, the dialogue had begun, the seeds of understanding sown. Each councilman was left to grapple with his inner demons, his own doubts and fears. Their journey towards acceptance or rejection of the new faith was emblematic of humanity's larger spiritual journey. A journey fraught with trials and tribulations but also brimming with the potential for divine enlightenment and salvation.

As Mary transcribed these encounters, she marveled at the interplay of cosmic forces and human determination. The apostles' trials were not merely earthly tribulations, but battles fought on multiple planes of existence. In the depths of her soul, Mary's faith was fortified, knowing that the apostles were not alone in their struggle. The divine hand guided their every step, empowering them to face the challenges of a world in need of salvation.

In the depths of the unseen realm, the battle between good and evil raged on. The angel and the Devil continued their relentless dialogue, each seeking to influence the unfolding events in their favor. The apostles, unaware of the cosmic forces at play, pressed forward with unwavering resolve. As I chronicled the journey of James, the brother of Jesus, I sensed the Devil's presence growing more pronounced. He seethed with resentment, his every move calculated to undermine the apostles' mission. He saw in James a formidable opponent, a pillar of strength and conviction who could rally the faithful with his unwavering faith. The Devil's whispers of doubt reached the ears of those around James, as he encountered resistance and skepticism from religious leaders and those who clung to tradition. But the angel, ever vigilant, countered with words of encouragement, reminding James of the miracles he had witnessed and the truth he carried within his heart. In one particularly pivotal moment, James stood before a crowd in the temple, his voice resounding with conviction. The Devil, seething with fury, sought to manipulate the religious leaders into turning against him. But the angel, ever watchful, infused James with an unyielding strength, enabling him to boldly proclaim the Gospel, even in the face of opposition. The clash between light and darkness escalated with every passing moment. The Devil's minions instigated unrest, sparking a revolt in Jerusalem that ultimately led to the city's devastating sacking by the Romans. Chaos and despair seemed to prevail, and the Devil reveled in the misery that his actions had wrought. But the angel's voice, though soft and subtle, resonated with unwavering hope. It reminded the apostles that even in the darkest of times, the light of Christ would prevail. It urged them to press forward, to endure the trials that lay ahead, for their mission was of divine origin and carried with it the promise of redemption. As my pen captured the events that unfolded, I felt a sense of urgency. The Devil's plans were cunning and intricate, woven with meticulous care. The battles between the angel and the Devil grew more intense, their arguments echoing through the unseen realm. In this saga of light and shadow, the reader bore witness to the tremendous power of faith and the resilience of the human spirit. The apostles, guided by the Holy Spirit and fortified by their guardian angels, faced trials and tribulations with unwavering resolve. And in their unwavering commitment, they became beacons of hope, spreading the message of salvation throughout the world.

Mary stood before the gathered believers, her eyes shining with reverence as she spoke of Matthew's sacred call to document the life and teachings of Jesus. "Matthew's journey led him to Jerusalem, the spiritual center of our faith," Mary began, her voice filled with awe. "Inspired by the Holy Spirit, he felt compelled to preserve the wisdom and love of our Lord in a written account." The congregation leaned in, eager to hear more about Matthew's mission and the importance of his Gospel. They knew that within those sacred scrolls lay the key to understanding the transformative power of Jesus's teachings. As Mary continued, she shared the challenges that Matthew and his companions faced in preserving the Gospel amidst a world resistant to change. "Matthew understood the weight of his responsibility," Mary explained, her voice tinged with urgency. "Religious authorities and rulers sought to suppress the message of Jesus, seeing it as a threat to their power." The flock nodded, aware of the opposition that awaited those who dared to challenge the established order. They understood that Matthew's pen became a shield against the forces seeking to silence the truth. In hushed tones, Mary recounted the perils faced by Matthew and his fellow disciples as they sought to protect the sacred scrolls from falling into the wrong hands. "Our enemies were relentless," Mary whispered, her voice filled with determination. "Matthew and the disciples clandestinely smuggled the scrolls out of Jerusalem, entrusting them to faithful believers who would carry them to distant lands." The congregation felt a shiver run down their spines, their hearts heavy with the sacrifices made to safeguard the Gospel. They knew the value of those scrolls, not just as written words, but as a vessel of hope for all who sought salvation. With fervor in her eyes, Mary spoke of Matthew's encounters with diverse cultures and individuals hungry for the message of Jesus. "Matthew's journey took him to distant lands, where he faced unique challenges and encountered different perspectives," Mary said, her voice filled with admiration. "But his unwavering conviction in the truth of Jesus's message allowed him to bridge cultural divides and touch the hearts of people from all walks of life." The congregation nodded in agreement, their spirits lifted by the universality of Jesus's teachings. They realized that the Gospel of Matthew could transcend barriers and speak to the deepest longings of the human soul. Mary's voice grew softer as she described the miracles that Matthew had witnessed, miracles that spoke of Jesus's divine nature. "Matthew saw blind eyes opened, the sick healed, and even the dead raised to life," Mary whispered, her voice filled with wonder. "These miracles affirmed the power and compassion of our Lord." As Mary spoke, the congregation could almost feel the presence of Jesus, the touch of His healing hands, and the overwhelming love that emanated from Him. The miracles became tangible, etched within their hearts. Mary's words took on a rhythmic cadence as she shared the parables that Matthew had skillfully woven into his Gospel.

While the council deliberated, the Apostle walked the streets, his heart burdened by the task before him. He had observed the growing divide amongst the people and the council's heated debates, realizing the enormity of the mission entrusted to him by Jesus. Suddenly, he found himself in a quiet, secluded corner of the marketplace. As he closed his eyes, he felt a presence. It was warm and comforting, like a gentle embrace. A figure appeared before him: an Angel representing the Holy Spirit. The Angel spoke, "Do not despair, for you are not alone in your mission. Remember the teachings of the Buddha: 'No one saves us but ourselves. We ourselves must walk the path.'" The Apostle, Matthew, comforted by these words, looked at the Angel. He was aware of the temptations the Devil had placed before the people and the Councilmen. He understood the power of the seven deadly sins and how they could sway the human heart. But he also knew the strength of the seven virtues and the transformative power of divine love. He nodded, his resolve strengthening, "I understand. I must continue to share Jesus' teachings of love, compassion, and forgiveness. It's not just about convincing others; it's about walking the path myself, living by example." In the mystical ethereal plane, the Devil saw this and scoffed, "Do you really think they will choose the difficult path of virtue over the tempting ease of sin?" The Angel, unperturbed, replied, "Every person has the capacity for both virtue and sin. But each also has the capacity for love, forgiveness, and transformation. They have the freedom to choose." And with those words, the Apostle felt a renewed sense of purpose. He understood that his mission was not just about preaching but also about embodying the virtues that Jesus taught. He realized that the road ahead would be difficult and fraught with challenges, but he was ready. He stepped back into the bustling marketplace, not with the aim to preach, but to show through his actions the power of divine love. He would demonstrate patience when met with anger, show kindness in the face of cruelty, offer forgiveness to those who wronged him. Through his actions, he would exemplify the power of Jesus' salvation, a beacon of divine love amidst the darkness. And thus, the stage was set. The struggle between the virtues and sins continued, reflected in every individual's choices and actions. But within that struggle lay the potential for transformation, for divine love to shine through, a testament to the salvation promised by Jesus.

Matthew's journey was just one chapter in this epic narrative of humanity's spiritual journey. As she called the congregation to their feet to pray at the opening of the service, she looked out onto the faces and saw in her spirit the troublesome thoughts that the devil used to destroy the progress of the Apostles and her works to bring salvation to all the souls that needed salvation by Jesus' grace. "The challenges we face are great, my dear brothers and sisters," Mary began, her voice filled with conviction. "But let us not forget the power that resides within us, the power of faith, the power of love, and the power of the Gospel that Matthew has entrusted to us." The flock gathered around Mary, their eyes searching for guidance and reassurance. They had witnessed the transformative impact of Matthew's Gospel and had felt the Holy Spirit move among them. "Though the devil seeks to sow doubt and division among us, we must remain steadfast," Mary continued, her words resolute. "We carry within us the living testament of Jesus's teachings, and it is our duty to share this message of hope, even in the face of persecution." As Mary spoke, the flock felt a surge of renewed determination. They remembered the miracles, the parables, and the wisdom of Jesus that had touched their lives. They understood that their faith was not meant to be hidden away but to be shared with the world. "We may face opposition and adversity," Mary declared, her voice rising with conviction, "but let us rise above it, united in our purpose. Let us build communities of believers, where the Gospel is not only read but lived out in our actions and interactions." The flock nodded, their spirits lifted by Mary's words. They were no longer a scattered group of believers; they were a united force, ready to face the challenges ahead. "As we go forth from this place," Mary concluded, her voice resolute, "let us carry the transformative power of Matthew's Gospel within us. Let it be a guiding light in our interactions with others, and let it be a source of strength as we face the machinations of the devil." With hearts aflame, the flock dispersed, each member filled with a renewed sense of purpose and an unwavering commitment to share the message of Jesus. They understood that through their collective efforts, the transformative power of faith would continue to spread, illuminating the darkness and bringing hope to a world in need.

And so, the saga continued, with Mary and the believers courageously facing the challenges ahead, their unwavering faith serving as a beacon of light in a world fraught with opposition. As they carried the teachings of Jesus within their hearts, they became agents of transformation, creating communities of love, unity, and unwavering devotion to the Gospel. Mary's eyes scanned the worried faces before her, her voice filled with determination. "Do not be disheartened by the opposition we face. The devil seeks to hinder our progress, but we shall overcome. Let the truth guide us, for it is a powerful shield against deception." Unbeknownst to the congregation, the devil watched from the shadows, his dark presence felt but not seen. As Mary's words resonated with the flock, the devil whispered his malevolent response, attempting to sow seeds of doubt and confusion. In the spiritual realm, the devil's voice echoed, taunting Mary and the believers. "Your efforts are futile, Mary. I will not let Matthew's Gospel take hold. I will sow seeds of doubt and division among those who follow his words." However, the flock, empowered by their faith and the presence of the Holy Spirit, remained steadfast. They could sense the spiritual warfare unfolding around them, but their hearts were fortified against the devil's deceptions. Gathered together in a place of worship, Mary and the believers engaged in deep discussions about the corruption that the devil was using to impede the spread of the Gospel. Their conversations were punctuated by moments of spiritual discernment, guided by the Holy Spirit. Mary's gaze swept across the room, her voice filled with conviction. "We must shine a light on the darkness that seeks to engulf us. Let us expose deceit and corruption, for the truth shall prevail." As the believers delved deeper into the mysteries surrounding the devil's minions, they could feel the subtle presence of the devil himself, attempting to disrupt their unity and sow discord.

A tremor of darkness filled the spiritual realm as the devil whispered in response to their discussions. "You are but a small flame in the face of my darkness. Your unity is fragile, and I will exploit it to my advantage." Yet, the believers remained undeterred, their hearts united by a common purpose. They recognized the devil's attempts to divide them and were fortified by their shared faith in Jesus. Mary and the flock found themselves confronted by the devil's minions, who sought to intimidate and silence their voices. But the power of the Holy Spirit emboldened them to stand firm against the enemy's attacks. Mary stood before the congregation, her voice steady as she addressed their fears. "We are engaged in a battle for truth, and we shall not falter. Stand firm, my dear brothers and sisters, for the Gospel of Matthew is a beacon of hope that cannot be extinguished."

In the spiritual realm, the devil sneered as he witnessed their determination, his voice reverberating through the flock, though they did not hear it audibly. The devil's presence darkened the spiritual realm as he whispered, "Your faith is admirable, but it is no match for my cunning and influence. I will strike at your weakest points and exploit your vulnerabilities." Yet, the flock remained unyielding, rooted in their faith and armed with the knowledge that the victory had already been won through Jesus's sacrifice.

Through their collective efforts, Mary and the flock began to unveil the corruption orchestrated by the devil and his minions. As they exposed the darkness, the light of truth pierced through, revealing the deep-rooted influence of the enemy. Mary's eyes sparkled with hope as she addressed the congregation. "We have come a long way, but our journey is not yet over. Let us continue to shed light on the devil's deceptions, for the truth has the power to set us free." In the spiritual realm, the devil seethed with anger as his carefully constructed plans crumbled beneath the weight of the believers' determination. The devil's whispers grew increasingly desperate as he realized his grip on the flock was slipping. "I will not be defeated. I will sow discord, create division, and turn hearts away from the truth." Yet, the believers, strengthened by their unwavering faith and the presence of the Holy Spirit, remained united. They understood the power of their collective voice and the truth they upheld, which would ultimately prevail over the darkness. And so, Mary and the congregation continued their journey, steadfast in their mission to spread the Gospel of Matthew and overcome the obstacles thrown in their path. As they pressed forward, guided by the Holy Spirit and fortified by their unwavering faith, the devil's schemes became but fleeting shadows in the face of the radiant truth they carried.

Chapter 11
John's Journey

The saga of John's journey and his unwavering dedication to spreading the message of Jesus would continue to unfold. Through persecution and trials, John remained resolute, drawing strength from his deep connection with Jesus and the loving support of his fellow disciples. The devil's attempts to hinder their mission only fueled their determination to bring the light of Christ to the darkest corners of the world.

As the saga of John's ministry unfolds, his legacy as the beloved disciple and the author of profound writings will shape the faith and beliefs of generations to come. His teachings will continue to inspire and guide believers, reminding them of the eternal hope found in Christ's sacrifice and the power of love to transform lives. The journey of John, the faithful disciple, reminds us that even in the face of adversity, the light of faith can triumph over darkness.

Through his unwavering commitment, his profound connection with Jesus, and the guidance of the Holy Spirit, John became a beacon of hope and love, illuminating a path for believers to follow. As we reflect on the saga of John's ministry, let us be inspired to live with unwavering faith, steadfast devotion, and an unyielding commitment to spreading the love of Christ. May his story encourage us to persevere in the face of trials, to stand firm against the schemes of the devil, and to embody the transformative power of Jesus' message in our lives. With the saga of John's ministry laid before us, the story continues to unfold, offering new chapters of triumph, revelation, and divine encounters.

As we embark on this journey, we anticipate the further expansion of John's legacy and the eternal impact of his unwavering faith. The arduous journey from Jerusalem to Samaria was filled with treacherous landscapes and wearying roads. Along the way, the disciples encountered a gathering of travelers, seeking solace and direction. James stepped forward, his voice infused with the divine authority bestowed upon him by the Holy Spirit. He spoke of Jesus' love and the transformative power of His message, his words resonating with the hearts of those who listened. As he finished, John joined him, their voices harmonizing as they sang hymns of praise and worship, their melodies carrying the promise of hope.

As John and James ventured into the land of Samaria, they encountered a rich tapestry of cultures, beliefs, and political tensions. The Samaritans, deeply rooted in their centuries-old religious practices, greeted the disciples with skepticism and resistance. The religious leaders saw them as interlopers, threatening the stability of their traditions. In the land of Samaria, a place steeped in deep-rooted traditions and political tensions, they encountered a rich tapestry of cultures and beliefs. John and James embarked on a formidable mission. They carried the light of Jesus' teachings to a people whose beliefs had been firmly entrenched for centuries. Their encounters with the Samaritans would test their faith and determination, while the angel by Mary's side provided guidance and insights into their journey.

Undeterred by the challenges they faced, John and James relied on the guidance of the Holy Spirit. Their words were infused with divine power, and their actions were marked by compassion and love. Miracles unfolded before the eyes of the Samaritans, touching the hearts of those who witnessed the transformative work of Jesus' grace. In the bustling marketplaces and gathering spaces, John and James engaged in profound debates with the Samaritans. They delved into philosophical discussions, challenging the long-held beliefs of the people. Through their dialogue, the disciples offered insights into the life and teachings of Jesus, illuminating a path of redemption and salvation.

Amidst the bustling city streets, the disciples engaged in fervent debates with the Samaritan religious leaders and philosophers. The clash of ideologies reverberated through the air, challenging the disciples' resolve. But the angel's whispers of wisdom, flowing to them from their guardian angel – the same angel that was relaying their episodes through Mary's pen – provided them with the strength and eloquence needed to defend the gospel's truth. They spoke of Jesus' teachings, the power of His miracles, and the boundless love He offered to all who believed. Mary, in Jerusalem, marveled at the stories of John and his brother, recorded with meticulous detail. She witnessed their encounters, their debates, and the powerful conversions that took place. The angel by her side provided spiritual insight and philosophical understanding, offering wisdom that deepened her appreciation for the impact of John's ministry.

One such encounter involved a Samaritan woman by the well. John's account reveals a poignant conversation that transcended cultural and societal barriers. He spoke of living water, a metaphor for the eternal life that Jesus offered to all who believed. The woman, moved by John's words and discerning his deep connection with the divine, experienced a profound transformation. She became an instrument of change, spreading the news of Jesus' teachings throughout her community. John's writings were filled with profound insights and spiritual truths. He penned the words of Jesus, "I am the way, the truth, and the life," conveying the essence of their message. His gospel resonated with the Samaritans, offering a path to reconciliation, unity, and a deeper understanding of God's love.

In the spectral realm, the Holy Spirit and the Devil resumed their discourse. Their dialogue was an eternal one, a conflict and concord of perspectives that echoed through the cosmos, shaping the course of human destiny. The Holy Spirit, a beacon of wisdom and compassion, began, "In their quest for happiness, mankind seeks to satiate desires and avoid suffering. However, transient pleasures and material wealth do not lead to true happiness. These are but ephemeral joys, fleeting and impermanent. True happiness, divine joy, comes from aligning one's will with the Divine Will, from surrendering to the boundless love of the Creator. It is this very surrender, this union with God, that John and the disciples seek to instill in the hearts of the people." The Devil, ever the contrarian, retorted, "Humans are inherently flawed, driven by their desires and passions. Even the disciples, in their moments of weakness, have faltered. How can you expect them to lead others to divine happiness when they themselves grapple with their own imperfections?" The Holy Spirit, unperturbed, responded, "It is precisely through their imperfections, their struggles, and their triumphs that they become beacons of hope for others. Their journey, fraught with challenges, serves as a testament to the transformative power of God's grace. Their unwavering faith, even in the face of adversity, is a testament to the strength of the human spirit, fueled by divine love." The Devil, always seeking to sow doubt, countered, "But what of those who turn away, who reject the teachings of Jesus and choose to walk a different path? How can they be redeemed?" The Holy Spirit, with an air of serenity, replied, "Every soul is on a journey, a quest for truth and meaning. Some may wander, some may falter, but the love of God is boundless, reaching out to embrace all who seek

Him. Redemption is always within reach for those who open their hearts to the divine embrace."

As the discourse between the Holy Spirit and the Devil continued, the saga of John's ministry and the disciples' journey played out on the earthly realm. Their unwavering commitment, their deep connection with Jesus, and the transformative power of their message would shape the course of history, leaving an indelible mark on the hearts and souls of countless believers. The journey of faith, filled with challenges and triumphs, serves as a testament to the enduring power of love, hope, and divine grace. As the saga unfolds, the story of John and the disciples reminds us of the eternal truth that love conquers all, that faith can move mountains, and that the light of Christ can illuminate even the darkest corners of the world.

In the physical world, the apostles Peter, James, John, and Paul moved through bustling marketplaces and serene countrysides, reaching out to communities far and wide. With the wisdom of the teachings they carried and the experiences they shared, they illuminated the path of righteousness to all they encountered. Miracles occurred at their hands, healing the sick and inspiring the weak of heart. Yet, they were not the originators of these divine phenomena but mere conduits of the Holy Spirit's power. The Devil, his guise as complex as the folds of human nature itself, had found fertile ground in the fears and doubts of those wavering on the precipice of belief. He whispered uncertainties into the hearts of men, creating divisions among the newly converted, stirring up confusion and dissent. Yet, the apostles stood unwavering amidst the chaos. They knew they were not merely fighting against flesh and blood, but against principalities and powers of the unseen world. The apostles, mindful of this truth, armed themselves not with physical weapons but with spiritual ones. Their armor was the wisdom they carried within their hearts, teachings that mirrored the wisdom of Marcus Aurelius, the Dalai Lama, and other philosophers of integrity, ethics, and happiness. They shielded themselves with the faith they had in the Divine's love and salvation. Paul wrote to the Ephesians, "Stand firm then, with the belt of truth buckled around your waist, with the breastplate of righteousness in place, and with your feet fitted with the readiness that comes from the gospel of peace. In addition to all this, take up the shield of faith, with which you can extinguish all the flaming arrows of the evil one." The Devil's deceptions were met with the apostles' steadfast faith and unwavering commitment to the path of righteousness. Each doubt sown was countered with a reaffirmation of faith; each fear invoked was silenced by the soothing words of divine assurance.

During this time, John, the beloved disciple of Jesus, found himself exiled on the island of Patmos. It was there that he received a profound vision, one that would become the last book of the Christian Bible, the Book of Revelation. In his vision, John saw the triumph of good over evil, the establishment of a new heaven and a new earth, the judgment of the wicked, and the reward of the righteous. This was a testament to the faith that no matter how dire the circumstances may appear, the Divine would prevail in the end. It was a vision as intricate and symbolic as it was inspiring. While some viewed the Revelation with fear and apprehension, many others saw it as a promise. It stood as an affirmation of the eventual victory of good over evil, an assurance that every tear would be wiped away, and that pain and suffering would be no more. The apostles carried this hope in their hearts as they journeyed forth, their spirits undaunted by the challenges they faced. Armed with the wisdom of Jesus and enlightened philosophers, and guided by the Holy Spirit, they carried the torch of faith, illuminating the path of righteousness for all those who sought the Divine.

Through this epic journey, this dialogue of duality between righteousness and temptation, they showcased the transformative power of Jesus' salvation. It was a testament to the enduring promise of hope, peace, and eternal happiness for all those who would choose the path of righteousness over the path of sin.

Chapter 12
The Vision of the End Times

Thus, as the struggle between the Holy Spirit and the Devil continued, the apostles' mission persevered. With each step, with every word spoken in the name of love and salvation, the message of Jesus spread further, lighting the way for those lost in darkness, and forever altering the spiritual landscape of humankind. Within the heart of Samaria, John and James continued their divine task. They traversed bustling marketplaces and sacred temples, engaging in deep conversations with the Samaritans. The disciples spoke of Jesus' love, His sacrifice, and the redemption that awaited those who believed in Him. The allure of their words drew crowds, their voices rising above the clamor of everyday life.

Yet, amidst the progress, challenges arose. The Devil's minions, working through the hearts of the Samaritans, stirred resentment and hostility towards the disciples. Tempers flared, and confrontations became more frequent. It was in these moments of turmoil that John and James leaned on their unshakeable faith, finding solace in the guidance of the angel. The disciples encountered one particular Samaritan philosopher, renowned for his skepticism and intellectual prowess.

The debates that ensued were fierce, with arguments ranging from the nature of God to the purpose of life itself. The Samaritan philosopher challenged the disciples at every turn, aiming to dismantle their beliefs and discredit their message.

However, not all who listened were receptive. The religious leaders of Samaria, threatened by the disciples' growing influence, sought to discredit them and their message. They spread false rumors and sowed seeds of doubt among the people, casting shadows of deception over the truth that John and James proclaimed. Undeterred, the disciples pressed on. They met with Samaritan families in their homes, breaking bread together and sharing stories of Jesus' teachings. The intimate settings allowed for deep connections to form, bridging the divide between Samaritans and Jews. Through their unwavering faith and the power of their testimonies, John and James kindled a spark of hope within the hearts of the Samaritans.

But John and James, filled with the Holy Spirit, stood their ground. They responded with grace, weaving together the wisdom imparted by Jesus and the insights gained from their own profound encounters with Him. The divine presence illuminated their words, penetrating the skeptic's heart and planting seeds of truth within his doubts. As the days turned into weeks, the Samaritans began to embrace the teachings of Jesus. They witnessed firsthand the transformative power of His love, and their hearts opened to the possibility of a new way of life. The shadows of deception that had clouded their minds gradually dissipated, replaced by the radiant light of truth.

Through Mary's diligent recording, the saga of John and James unfolded. The trials they faced, the triumphs they celebrated, and the souls they touched were etched into the annals of history. Each encounter, each debate, was a testament to the unyielding faith and unwavering dedication of the disciples, as they carried the torch of Jesus' message into the heart of Samaria.

In the depths of his solitude, John's spirit remained unbroken. He knew that even in the darkest of times, the light of Jesus' love would guide him. It was during his time of isolation that something extraordinary unfolded: the revelation. In the stillness of the prison cell, John's senses became attuned to the spiritual realm. The veil between the physical and the divine was lifted, allowing him to witness the heavenly realms and receive profound visions. He beheld scenes of great cosmic significance, filled with symbols, imagery, and messages that would shape the future of the Christian faith. With quill in hand and the guidance of the Holy Spirit, John began to document his revelations. In the form of letters, he penned the seven epistles, addressing the churches in Asia Minor. Through these letters, he provided guidance, encouragement, and warnings to the communities of believers, urging them to remain steadfast in their faith despite the trials they faced.

Mary, in Jerusalem, marveled at the accounts of John's visions. The angel by her side offered insights into the symbolism and significance of the revelations. Together, they pondered the profound messages contained within the visions and the impact they would have on the growing Christian community. One of the key visions John received was that of the glorified Christ. He described a figure clothed in radiant white, with eyes aflame, souls on fire, and a voice like rushing waters. His face shone like the sun, and His countenance radiated both authority and love. This majestic vision affirmed Jesus' divinity and His eternal reign. Another vision revealed the cosmic battle between good and evil. John witnessed the great dragon, symbolizing the forces of darkness, engaged in a fierce conflict with the heavenly hosts. The vision spoke of the ultimate triumph of God's kingdom over the forces of evil, filling the hearts of believers with hope and assurance. The angel by John's side interpreted the visions, revealing their profound spiritual truths. The symbolism of the seven churches, the seals, the trumpets, and the bowls all carried deep meaning, signifying the challenges, victories, and ultimate redemption that lay ahead for the Church.

In their discussions, Mary and the angel recognized the significance of the revelation. They saw it as a beacon of hope, a message of perseverance and endurance for the believers in the face of persecution. The revelation served as a reminder that God's divine plan was unfolding, and His promises would be fulfilled. As John continued to write, he delved deeper into the mysteries of the revelation. The visions of the four living creatures, the twenty-four elders, and the heavenly worship painted a vivid picture of the glory and majesty of God's presence. The scrolls, the seals, and the Lamb of God revealed the divine plan of redemption, offering solace and guidance to the early Christian community. The saga of John's revelation on the island of Patmos was only just beginning. The messages, symbols, and prophecies he recorded would become a cornerstone of Christian eschatology, inviting believers throughout the ages to seek wisdom, discernment, and faith in the face of adversity.

In the astral realm, the Holy Spirit, embodying a serene presence of grace, addressed the Adversary, "Despite your efforts to sway individuals away from the path of righteousness, the power of divine love proves stronger. The message of Jesus, of compassion, forgiveness, and love, rings true in many hearts, inspiring individuals to rise above their fears and challenges." The Adversary, emanating a cold aura, retorted, "My influence is still strong. Many still succumb to their fears, their prejudices, their selfish desires." "Yes," conceded the Holy Spirit, "Yet, each individual who chooses love over hatred, forgiveness over resentment, compassion over apathy, is a victory for the divine. These are the seeds of change, the sparks that can ignite a flame of transformation."

In the physical realm, the apostles continued their mission with renewed vigor. They traversed through lands far and wide, braving harsh weather, hostile crowds, and intense fatigue. Yet, the divine fire within them remained unquenchable, their spirits resilient. Simon, confronted with a mob of angry villagers, spoke calmly, his words radiating an undeniable sincerity, "Fear not the message we bring. We speak not of punishment, but of salvation. We speak not of dominance, but of love. The path we tread is not easy, yet the peace and joy it promises are everlasting." In another part of the world, Thomas, despite being ridiculed and shunned, remained unyielding. "Doubt, question, and challenge our teachings," he encouraged, "But do not dismiss them out of fear or ignorance. Seek the truth, and you shall find it." Their words, their actions, their unyielding faith served as a living testament to the teachings they propagated. And though many chose to remain in the comforting grip of their old beliefs, there were others who, moved by the apostles' unyielding faith and compassion, began to question, to seek, to believe.

Dialogues of Duality: In the unseen astral realm, a discourse of great significance was taking place. In the grand scale of cosmic time, this spiritual battle between the Holy Spirit and the Adversary, this war of ideologies being fought in the hearts of humans, was but a fleeting moment. Yet, each victory for love, each triumph for faith, was a significant step forward in the spiritual evolution of humankind. The battle raged on, the lines drawn not in sand or stone, but in the human heart. For the apostles, guided by the Holy Spirit, it was not a battle against an external enemy, but an internal struggle within each individual, a choice between love and fear, faith and doubt, selflessness and selfishness. Despite the immense challenges, the apostles carried on, their spirits fueled by the love of the Divine, their resolve solidified by their unwavering faith. And in every heart that chose love, in every soul that found faith, they found their victory.

Dialogues of Duality: In the unseen astral realm, a discourse of great significance was taking place. The Holy Spirit and the Devil engaged in a metaphysical dialogue, the weight of their words reverberating through the cosmos. The Holy Spirit, a radiant beacon of divine love, began, "In all beings, there is the potential for good and evil, for light and dark. This duality exists not as a curse, but as an opportunity for growth, for understanding, and for compassion. When faced with adversity, man has the opportunity to choose love over hate, forgiveness over resentment, integrity over deceit. This is the path of righteousness that Jesus proclaimed."

The Devil, embodiment of the seven cardinal sins, retorted, "But is it not easier to surrender to the darkness, to indulge in the pleasures of the flesh and the ego? Is it not simpler to follow the path of least resistance than to struggle against one's natural desires?"

"The path of righteousness is not easy," the Holy Spirit replied, "but it is fulfilling. For in the struggles, in the challenges, man discovers his true strength, his capacity for love, and his connection to the divine. While the temptations of the flesh may offer transient pleasure, they do not satiate the soul's longing for true happiness and purpose."

The Devil, with a sly grin, countered, "Yet, so many fall to my temptations, choosing the fleeting joys of material wealth, power, and hedonism. Does this not prove that man's nature is inherently flawed, prone to sin and corruption?"

The Holy Spirit, unperturbed, responded, "Every fall, every misstep, is an opportunity for redemption. It is in recognizing their flaws and seeking forgiveness that individuals experience profound spiritual growth. Your temptations may lead some astray, but they also provide the contrast necessary for others to recognize the true value of right-eousness, love, and compassion."

The Devil, ever the skeptic, questioned, "But what of those who never find their way back, those who remain lost in the shadows of their own desires?"

The Holy Spirit, with infinite patience, replied, "No soul is ever truly lost. The divine spark within each individual is eternal, and while the journey back to the light may be long and fraught with challenges, the potential for redemption is always present. The love of the Divine is boundless and unconditional, ever waiting to embrace those who seek it."

As their discourse continued, the saga of the apostles' mission on Earth played out. Their unwavering commitment, their deep connection with Jesus, and the transformative power of their message served as a testament to the enduring power of love, hope, and faith. Despite the challenges and temptations, they persevered, shining a light on the path of righteousness for all to follow. In the end, the dialogue between the Holy Spirit and the Devil highlighted the eternal dance of duality, the balance of light and dark, good and evil, that exists within the universe. It served as a reminder that while the challenges may be great, the potential for love, redemption, and spiritual growth is even greater. Through the trials and triumphs, the message remains clear: Love conquers all, faith can move mountains, and the light of righteousness will always shine through the darkness.

Chapter 13
The book of Revelation,

T he Revelation's Promise:

John's Revelation was a beacon of hope amidst the spiritual turbulence, providing reassurance to those grappling with the fear of the unknown. The imagery, though complex and often daunting, bore a promise of divine triumph over earthly tribulations. The seven-headed beast, the ominous horsemen, and the mark of the beast - these symbols of tribulation were formidable. Yet, they were but precursors to the eventual victory of the Divine, a victory signifying the dawn of a new era of peace, love, and righteousness. This hope, embedded in the heart of the prophecy, bolstered the spirits of the believers, helping them endure the adversities they faced.

At the heart of the Revelation's message was the promise of a new heaven and a new earth, where the Divine dwells among people, where there is no more death, mourning, crying, or pain. This promise held a profound appeal, echoing humanity's age-old yearning for an end to suffering and the onset of eternal peace and happiness. Despite the growing acceptance of Jesus' teachings and the proliferation of Christian communities, the struggle between the Holy Spirit and the Adversary remained. The Devil, ever the deceiver, continued his attempts to mislead, to sow discord, and to breed doubt. He manipulated the seven cardinal sins to serve his purpose, exploiting humanity's vulnerabilities to veer them off the path of righteousness. Yet, with every adversity, the believers' faith only grew stronger. The Holy Spirit, working through the apostles, helped them discern truth from falsehood, guiding them towards righteousness. The strength of their faith served as a testament to the transformative power of Jesus' salvation, providing a beacon of hope for those still trapped in the shadows of doubt and fear.

As the apostles journeyed forth, they carried with them the wisdom of Jesus, the teachings of enlightened philosophers, and the promise of the Revelation. They were the bearers of a message that promised salvation, happiness, and an upright life for those who accepted Jesus' divine grace. In this epic spiritual struggle, they served as examples of resilience, compassion, and unwavering faith, embodying the essence of the divine message they sought to spread. This was their legacy, a testament to the power of faith, the promise of redemption, and the enduring hope for a world guided by love, peace, and divine righteousness. As the story unfolds, let us journey alongside John, diving deeper into the realms of heavenly visions and spiritual revelations. May we find inspiration, encouragement, and a renewed sense of purpose as we witness the unfolding of God's divine plan through the eyes of the beloved apostle.

Penned by John during his exile on the island of Patmos, the Book of Revelation stands as a remarkable testament to divine revelation. It is a tapestry of vivid and symbolic imagery, filled with prophecies, warnings, and promises that ignite the imagination and captivate the soul. The opening chapters of Revelation offer a glimpse into the state of the seven churches in Asia Minor. John, acting as a divine messenger, addresses each church, commending their faithfulness, rebuking their shortcomings, and urging them to persevere in the face of persecution. The messages serve as timeless reminders of the importance of faith, repentance, and spiritual endurance.

As the book unfolds, John unveils a series of visions that transport the reader into the realms of heavenly mysteries and eschatological events. One of the most dramatic moments comes with the opening of the seven seals. As each seal is broken, a powerful symbol emerges, revealing events that will shape the course of human history. The opening of the first seal unleashes a white horse, its rider bearing a bow and wearing a crown. This image represents conquest, signaling the rise of powerful leaders and the unfolding of geopolitical events. Mary, in Jerusalem, contemplates the significance of this vision and ponders how it relates to the challenges faced by the early Christian community. The second seal brings forth a red horse, its rider holding a great sword. This symbolizes war and bloodshed, representing the conflicts that will ravage the earth. Mary contemplates the devastating impact of war and its implications for believers, reflecting on the call to peace and the pursuit of righteousness in the midst of chaos. With the opening of the third seal, a black horse appears, its rider holding scales. This vision speaks of famine and economic hardships, foretelling the struggles that will plague humanity. Mary meditates on the importance of stewardship, justice, and compassionate care for the marginalized in times of scarcity and deprivation. The fourth seal reveals a pale horse, ridden by Death, with Hades following closely behind. This chilling image embodies death and its conquest over mankind, a stark reminder of the fragility of human existence. Mary contemplates the brevity of life and the urgency to embrace the hope of eternal salvation. As the visions progress, John unveils the cataclysmic events known as the seven trumpets. Each trumpet blast heralds a divine judgment, bringing destruction and upheaval upon the earth. From devastating plagues to celestial disturbances, the trumpets amplify the message of divine intervention and the need for repentance.

One of the most awe-inspiring moments comes with the seventh trumpet, as the heavenly sanctuary is opened, revealing the Ark of the Covenant. This signifies God's presence and His ultimate triumph over evil. Mary reflects on the power of God's deliverance and the promise of a new covenant sealed through the sacrifice of Jesus Christ. The culmination of the Book of Revelation comes with the vision of the woman and the dragon. The woman, adorned with the sun, moon, and stars, symbolizes the faithful people of God. The dragon, a representation of Satan, wages war against the woman and her off-spring. Mary contemplates the cosmic battle between good and evil and the assurance that God's ultimate victory is certain. As the saga of Revelation draws to a close, the angel by Mary's side shares profound insights into the spiritual significance of these visions. They discuss the metaphorical nature of the symbols, the challenges faced by the early Church, and the timeless relevance of the messages contained within the book. Mary gains a deeper understanding of the trials and tribulations faced by believers, as well as the assurance that God's providence and sovereignty are ever present. She contemplates the call to remain faithful, to persevere in the face of persecution, and to hold fast to the hope of Christ's return.

Mary, in Jerusalem, sat in deep contemplation, her mind filled with the visions and symbols of the Book of Revelation. Her conversations with the angel had illuminated the profound truths embedded within the prophetic text, stirring a mix of awe, anticipation, and concern within her heart. As Mary sought further understanding, the angel began to unravel the symbolism and significance of the visions that unfolded before John on the island of Patmos. They delved into the seals, trumpets, and bowls of wrath, exploring the intricate tapestry of divine judgment, spiritual warfare, and ultimate redemption.

One of the most perplexing visions in Revelation is the depiction of the beast rising from the sea. The angel explained that the beast symbolized earthly powers, political systems, and ideologies that oppose God's kingdom. Mary shuddered at the thought of the immense influence and destructive nature of these forces, which sought to deceive and lead people astray. Amidst the darkness, however, the angel revealed the triumph of the Lamb. Jesus Christ, portrayed as the victorious Lamb, would overcome the forces of evil and establish His eternal kingdom. Mary found solace in this powerful imagery, recognizing that even in the midst of turmoil, God's ultimate plan for redemption and restoration would prevail.

The angel also shed light on the role of the seven churches in Revelation. They represented not only specific historical churches in Asia Minor but also symbolized various spiritual conditions and challenges faced by believers throughout history. Mary realized that the letters to the churches were not merely for a specific time and place but carried timeless messages of encouragement, correction, and hope.

In the unseen realm, two entities, embodiments of the divine and the diabolical, found themselves in a discourse, a celestial trial of values and principles. The celestial advocate of the divine message, strengthened by a reservoir of wisdom gathered from the ages, squared off against the devil's advocate, the orchestrator of the seven cardinal sins, and the embodiment of all that stood against the divine message of salvation.

The celestial advocate began the discourse, his voice echoing through the cosmic realm, "For those who seek joy and purpose, the path lies not in temporal pleasures but in inner contentment. Look upon the humble water bearer who rejoices not in the gold coins but in the smiles of those he quenches. Such is the essence of real happiness, not an external acquisition, but an inner realization."

In response, the devil's advocate sneered, casting a shadow of cynicism over the spiritual dialogue, "Yet, is it not the nature of mankind to desire more, to lust for power, and to bask in the vanity of superiority? The humble water bearer, does he not yearn for a life of luxury? Is it not a fool's dream to seek joy in the act of selfless giving?"

Chapter 14
The Path is Illuminated

T he celestial advocate, unperturbed by the devil's advocate's skepticism, replied, "It is true that many are ensnared by the trappings of materialism and the allure of worldly pleasures. But true joy, the kind that permeates the soul and endures beyond fleeting moments, is found in the act of giving, in the warmth of genuine connection, and in the peace of a contented heart. The water bearer may occasionally dream of riches, but his true wealth lies in the difference he makes in the lives of those he serves."

The devil's advocate, ever the cynic, countered, "But what of ambition? Is it not ambition that drives progress, innovation, and prosperity? Are those who chase their dreams and seek to elevate their status not also deserving of admiration?"

The celestial advocate, with wisdom and grace, responded, "Ambition, in itself, is not inherently flawed. It is the intention behind the ambition that determines its virtue. Ambition driven by a desire to serve, uplift, and create a positive impact is commendable. However, ambition rooted in greed, envy, or the desire for domination leads one astray. True progress is measured not by the heights one attains, but by the lives one uplifts along the way."

The devil's advocate, seeking to sow doubt, posited, "Yet, in the grand tapestry of existence, do individual actions even matter? In a universe so vast, are human deeds not mere drops in an endless ocean?"

The celestial advocate, with a serene smile, replied, "Each drop contributes to the ocean's vastness. Every act, no matter how small, ripples through time and space, affecting the whole. It is the collective choices, the sum of individual actions, that shape the course of destiny. Every deed rooted in love, compassion, and righteousness adds to the light that dispels the darkness."

As the dialogue continued, it became evident that this was more than just a debate between two opposing entities. It was a reflection of the eternal struggle between light and dark, good and evil, that played out in the hearts and minds of every individual. The choices made, the paths chosen, would determine the trajectory of souls, communities, and ultimately, the fate of humanity

The celestial advocate, emanating a calm and serene aura, replied, "The essence of humanity is complex, interwoven with desires and aspirations. However, the true nature of the soul is to seek connection, love, and purpose. While the water bearer may momentarily yearn for luxury, the depth of his joy is derived from the purity of his service. Temporal pleasures are fleeting, but the contentment drawn from selfless acts endures."

Unfazed, the celestial advocate responded, "Ambition in itself is not detrimental. It is the intent behind it that determines its nature. Ambition fueled by compassion, purpose, and love elevates the soul. But when driven by greed, envy, or pride, it can lead one astray. True success is measured not by material acquisitions, but by the lives touched, the hearts healed, and the souls uplifted."

The devil's advocate smirked, "Yet, the world celebrates the wealthy, the powerful, often overlooking the quiet contributions of the humble. Is this not a testament to the allure of worldly success?"

The celestial advocate, with a gentle smile, responded, "The world may momentarily applaud material achievements, but the annals of time remember acts of kindness, courage, and love. The whispers of the humble water bearer's deeds, though seemingly insignificant, ripple through eternity, touching souls in ways unimaginable."

The devil's advocate, attempting one last challenge, said, "But amidst the chaos of life, the challenges, the trials, how can one consistently choose the path of righteousness? Is it not easier to succumb to temptation, to take the path of least resistance?"

The celestial advocate, with unwavering conviction, replied, "The journey of life is fraught with challenges and temptations. Yet, with every choice to embrace love over hate, compassion over apathy, and truth over deceit, the soul evolves, drawing closer to its divine essence. The path of righteousness, though arduous, is illuminated by the eternal light of divine grace, guiding all who choose to walk upon it."

With that, the celestial discourse, a testament to the eternal struggle between light and darkness, virtue and vice, continued, echoing through the realms of existence, reminding all of the timeless truths of love, faith, and divine purpose.

For in the struggles, in the challenges, man discovers his true strength, his capacity for love, and his connection to the divine. While the temptations of the flesh may offer transient pleasure, they do not satiate the soul's longing for true happiness and purpose."

The Devil, with a sly grin, countered, "Yet, so many fall to my temptations, choosing the fleeting joys of material wealth, power, and hedonism. Does this not prove that man's nature is inherently flawed, prone to sin and corruption?"

The Holy Spirit, unperturbed, responded, "Every fall, every misstep, is an opportunity for redemption. It is in recognizing their flaws and seeking forgiveness that individuals experience profound spiritual growth. Your temptations may lead some astray, but they also provide the contrast necessary for others to recognize the true value of righteousness, love, and compassion."

The Devil, ever the skeptic, questioned, "But what of those who never find their way back, those who remain lost in the shadows of their own desires?"

The Holy Spirit, with infinite patience, replied, "No soul is ever truly lost. The divine spark within each individual is eternal, and while the journey back to the light may be long and fraught with challenges, the potential for redemption is always present. The love of the Divine is boundless and unconditional, ever waiting to embrace those who seek it."

As their discourse continued, the saga of the apostles' mission on Earth played out. Their unwavering commitment, their deep connection with Jesus, and the transformative power of their message served as a testament to the enduring power of love, hope, and faith. Despite the challenges and temptations, they persevered, shining a light on the path of righteousness for all to follow.

In the end, the dialogue between the Holy Spirit and the Devil highlighted the eternal dance of duality, the balance of light and dark, good and evil, that exists within the universe. It served as a reminder that while the challenges may be great, the potential for love, redemption, and spiritual growth is even greater. Through the trials and triumphs, the message remains clear: Love conquers all, faith can move mountains, and the light of righteousness will always shine through the darkness.

Chapter 15
Discourse of Truth

U ndeterred by the cynicism, the celestial advocate continued, drawing upon the wisdom of ancient philosophers, "Emperor and philosopher Marcus Aurelius believed in the virtue of integrity. 'Never esteem anything as an advantage that will make you break your word or lose your self-respect.' To lead an upright life, to find true happiness and contentment, one must adhere to one's principles. Integrity forms the bedrock of human character, and the lack of it is the harbinger of chaos and misery."

The devil's advocate, driven by his mission to sow doubt, countered, "What is integrity but a shackle binding mankind's true potential? Is it not an excuse for the weak, a reason for the underprivileged to remain so? The survival of the fittest requires one to adapt, to change, to mold their principles as per their needs. Why should mankind limit its potential in the name of integrity?"

This dialogue, this battle of ideas, continued, echoing through the spiritual realm, a celestial debate watched by the cosmic jury of stars. Yet, amidst this discourse, the celestial advocate stood unwavering, his conviction unshaken. He continued his argument, drawing upon the teachings of Jesus, "The path to salvation, to eternal life, lies in love, in forgiveness. It is in understanding that every soul, despite its past sins, has the potential for redemption. It is not about the pursuit of pleasure or power, but about living a life of love and service."

The devil's advocate, hearing these words, fell silent. For all his cynicism, for all his manipulations, he couldn't refute the transformative power of love, the promise of redemption, and the hope of salvation. The discourse ended, not with a triumphant declaration, but with the profound silence of realization. The celestial advocate had not just won an argument; he had rekindled the light of faith, hope, and love in the cosmic arena.

The celestial advocate, seizing the silence, deepened his discourse. He drew from the profound wisdom of the Buddha, "Suffering is a part of life, an essential aspect of existence. Desire fuels this suffering, and the cessation of desire brings about the end of suffering. But, there is a difference between worldly desires and the desire for righteousness. The desire to live a virtuous life, to strive towards salvation, this is a desire that liberates, not binds."

Contrarily, the devil's advocate shot back, "Suffering and desire are intertwined, inseparable. Why seek to end desire when it is desire that makes life worth living? Why seek salvation when it means to suppress one's natural instincts, one's desires? The joy in life is to experience, to desire, to strive. Why trade this for salvation?"

Drawing inspiration from the Dalai Lama, the celestial advocate continued, "Change is the law of life. To resist change is to resist life itself. Fear of the unknown, resistance to change, these are the shackles that prevent us from reaching our potential, from embracing our destiny. The power of compassion, the ability to empathize, to understand, and to love, this is what truly leads to happiness, joy, and an upright life."

In contrast, the devil's advocate argued, "Change, like desire, is a double-edged sword. It can bring joy as well as sorrow. Why encourage change when it can lead to suffering? Is it not better to maintain the status quo, to cling to the known, the familiar?"

With each exchange, the celestial advocate unveiled the deceptive machinations of the devil's advocate. He highlighted the virtues of faith, compassion, integrity, and change, elucidating how these principles led to true happiness and salvation. In contrast, the devil's advocate's arguments exposed his intent to maintain his dominion over the souls, perpetuating their suffering by promoting fear, resistance to change, and submission to worldly desires. But as the celestial advocate continued to voice the divine message, drawing upon the profound wisdom of philosophers, spiritual leaders, and the teachings of Jesus, the celestial arena was lit with the glow of truth. This truth, vibrant and enlightening, overwhelmed the cynicism and deceit of the devil's advocate, heralding a resounding victory for the celestial advocate. The discourse culminated not just in the victory of the celestial advocate, but in the triumph of truth over deceit, of love over fear, of faith over doubt. It served as a reaffirmation of the promise of salvation and the transformative power of the divine message, a beacon of hope for all those struggling in their spiritual journey.

The celestial dialogue, echoing through the spiritual realm, became a testament to the enduring power of truth, love, and faith, the cornerstones of salvation.

As the dialogue between the celestial advocate and the devil's advocate ensued, the unfolding of the Seven Seals of Revelation marked the progression of their celestial discourse. The First Seal, as it broke, released the white horse of conquest, symbolizing the spread of the divine message. The apostles, guided by the Holy Spirit, embarked on their journey, their words touching hearts, enlightening minds, sparking the first surge of faith among humanity. When the Second Seal ruptured, the red horse of war emerged, epitomizing the spiritual warfare ensuing between the forces of good and evil, in the hearts of mankind and the spiritual realm. The Third Seal was opened, and the black horse of famine took flight, a representation of spiritual hunger, of souls yearning for the divine message, a testament to the growing influence of the Holy Spirit. The Fourth Seal was broken, and the pale horse of death was unleashed, a reminder of the mortality of flesh but the immortality of the spirit, emphasizing the eternal nature of the divine message. The Final Seals and the Divine Promise:

As the Fifth Seal unraveled, the souls of martyrs appeared, crying for justice. These were the faithful who had suffered for their belief, a symbol of their unwavering faith in the face of adversity, their sacrifices illuminating the path to salvation. The Sixth Seal opened, heralding cosmic disturbances, a symbol of the disruptive power of the divine message, shaking the foundations of old beliefs, paving the way for the new faith. Then came the silence before the Seventh Seal, an anticipatory pause that amplified the magnitude of the forthcoming revelation. Finally, as the Seventh Seal was broken, the silence was shattered by the trumpet of angels, a resounding affirmation of the divine promise. The final seal revealed the triumph of the divine message, the victory of faith over fear, love over hatred, truth over deceit. In the celestial arena, the triumph of the celestial advocate was mirrored in the breaking of the Seven Seals, each signifying a victory of the divine message, each a step forward in the journey of salvation. The unfolding of the Seals and the celestial dialogue wove a tale of faith, struggle, and triumph, a testament to the enduring power of the divine message.

In the ethereal realm, the celestial advocate and the devil's advocate observed the breaking of the First Seal. A rider on a white horse, holding a bow, was released. He wore a victor's crown and rode forth as a conqueror, hell-bent on conquest. The angel looked at this unfolding vision, a sense of affirmation radiating from him. "See, this is the divine mission manifesting. The white horse symbolizes purity and righteousness. Its rider, armed with a bow, represents the apostles, who are commissioned to conquer not through violence but through the power of the divine word. They are sent forth to conquer hearts and minds, to convert souls, to spread the word of God across the lands."

As the Second Seal broke, a red horse emerged. Its rider held a sword, given the power to take peace from the earth and make people kill each other. The angel, unperturbed, explained, "This red horse symbolizes the spiritual conflict that ensues when truth encounters deception. It is not an incitement of physical violence, but rather a metaphor for the spiritual warfare that rages in the hearts of mankind, a clash between faith and doubt, truth and falsehood."

When the Third Seal was opened, a black horse appeared. Its rider held a pair of scales in his hand, symbolizing scarcity and imbalance. The angel acknowledged, "The black horse represents the spiritual hunger that arises in souls yearning for truth. The scales held by its rider signify the need for balance, a reminder to humanity about the importance of spiritual nourishment, of seeking divine truth amidst the distractions of worldly desires."

With the breaking of the Fourth Seal, a pale horse emerged. Its rider was named Death, and Hades was following close behind him. The angel elucidated, "This pale horse symbolizes the mortality of the flesh and the immortality of the spirit. It is a profound reminder that while the physical body may perish, the soul lives on, embarking on a journey of divine ascension. Death, therefore, is not an end but a transition, a passage from the temporal to the eternal."

As the fifth seal was opened, the celestial advocate beheld the souls of those who had been slain because of the Word of God. They cried out for justice and were given white robes and told to wait a little longer. "The cry of the martyrs," the angel intoned, "is the echo of profound faith, a testament to their unwavering belief in the divine truth. These souls, symbolized by the white robes, have sanctified themselves through their sacrifice. Yet, they are asked to wait, for the divine plan unfolds in its own time, and every soul must find its path in this divine chronology."

Upon the breaking of the sixth seal, there were great cosmic disturbances. The sun turned black, the moon became like blood, and the stars fell from the sky. Every mountain and island was moved from its place. The celestial advocate, showing no fear, calmly elucidated the celestial chaos. "These cosmic disturbances represent a profound spiritual shift. The darkening sun, the blood-red moon, and falling stars are metaphors for the shaking of old beliefs, the upheaval of established truths, and the dislodging of complacency. It signifies the arrival of a transformative spiritual awakening."

When the seventh seal was opened, there was silence in heaven for about half an hour. Then, an angel carrying the seal of the living God descended. "The opening of the seventh seal marks the culmination of the divine plan," the angel expounded. "The silence that ensues is a hallowed moment of divine anticipation, a pause before the unfolding of God's ultimate design. The seal of the living God symbolizes the divine imprint on creation, a testament to God's eternal presence."

Throughout these revelations, the devil's advocate, observing in silence, tried to seed doubt and confusion. Yet, in the face of divine truth, his efforts were futile. The path of salvation, marked by these seven seals, was undeniably laid out, calling humanity towards faith, introspection, and the embrace of divine love.

The celestial advocate directed their gaze toward a vast multitude from every tribe of the sons of Israel. "These," he indicated, "are the 144,000 who have been sealed with the Seal of the Living God. They represent a symbolic number, signifying the countless faithful who choose the path of righteousness, marked by their dedication to divine will." In this assembly, the advocate saw souls cleansed and prepared for divine service. They bore the spiritual seal, protected from the coming tribulations, their hearts marked with the profound love for the Divine.

Chapter 16
A Multitude of Believers

Suddenly, a multitude that no one could number appeared. They were from every nation, tribe, people, and language. Dressed in white robes, with palm branches in their hands, they praised God with a loud voice. "The great multitude represents the entirety of the redeemed," the advocate explained. "The white robes symbolize their spiritual purity, achieved through faith and the transformative power of Divine love. Their unison praise symbolizes the unity of humanity under Divine grace."

As the seal narrative came to an end, a golden censer filled with incense was offered up, symbolizing the prayers of the saints. This marked the beginning of the sounding of the seven trumpets. "These trumpets herald significant events, each marking a different aspect of the divine plan," the angel remarked. "They echo the divine will across the dimensions, a call to humanity to awaken to the spiritual realities." The devil's advocate watched, as the truth of the divine plan illuminated the spiritual realm. His once formidable stronghold was wavering, slowly eroded by the faith of the redeemed and the unfolding of the Divine plan.

With the first trumpet's call, hail and fire mixed with blood descended, torching a third of the Earth, trees, and all green grass. "This," said the celestial advocate, "marks the beginning of a spiritual awakening, a call to return to divine roots. It represents the destructive force of spiritual negligence."

The second trumpet summoned a massive mountain, ablaze, cast into the sea. A third of the sea turned into blood, its creatures perished, and ships were destroyed. "This signifies a disruption of life's harmonious rhythm when humanity loses its moral compass."

With the third trumpet's sound, a star named Wormwood fell from the heavens, poisoning a third of the Earth's waters. "Wormwood symbolizes the bitter consequences of straying from the divine path."

Finally, the fourth trumpet summoned darkness, a third of the sun, moon, and stars were struck, losing their light. "This alludes to the spiritual darkness that ensues when divine guidance is ignored," explained the celestial advocate.

Just as the fourth trumpet ended its toll, an eagle flying in mid-heaven cried out, "Woe, woe, woe to those who dwell on the earth, at the blasts of the other trumpets that the three angels are about to blow!" "These woes serve as warnings, a call for repentance and return to the divine path," clarified the advocate. The devil's advocate observed the proceedings, his countenance clouded. He felt the undeniable power of the divine plan unfolding, each trumpet sounding the toll of his influence on mankind. But his resolve was unbroken; he prepared to counter the divine will, to tempt and lead astray as many as he could.

With the sounding of the fifth trumpet, a star fell from the heavens onto the earth, entrusted with the key to the bottomless pit. Upon opening it, smoke filled the skies, blocking out the sun, and from this smoke, emerged locusts, granted the power to torment. "This star," clarified the celestial advocate, "is a fallen angel, and these locusts are symbolic of the false prophets who lead people astray with their tormenting lies." The devil's advocate smirked, recognizing the metaphor for his own agents of chaos, sowing seeds of doubt and division among the people. Yet, as he watched the narrative unfold, he couldn't help but notice that despite the pain and chaos, many still clung to their faith, their love for God unshaken.

As the sixth trumpet sounded, a voice commanded the release of the four angels bound at the great river Euphrates. The angels, who had been prepared for this hour, day, month, and year, were released to kill a third of mankind. "This," said the celestial advocate solemnly, "is a call to awareness. It signifies the danger of spiritual warfare, the consequences of aligning oneself with darkness." The devil's advocate could feel the strain, the battle of good versus evil intensifying. He understood, as the celestial advocate spoke, that every action taken, every decision made, was another step in this spiritual journey, and the fate of souls hung in the balance.

After the sixth trumpet, a mighty angel came down from heaven, robed in a cloud, with a rainbow over his head. He held a small scroll, unsealed, in his hand. The celestial advocate explained, "This scroll contains God's plan for the future, His divine will that shall come to pass. It's a reminder that amidst the trials and tribulations, God's plan remains unwavering." The devil's advocate could only watch, a strange mix of anticipation and apprehension within him, as he awaited the sound of the seventh trumpet.

Finally, the seventh trumpet sounded, bringing a sense of finality, a promise of closure. There were loud voices in heaven proclaiming, "The kingdom of the world has become the kingdom of our Lord and of His Christ, and He shall reign forever and ever." "This," said the celestial advocate, "is the culmination of it all, the victory of

God's kingdom. It signifies the end of the Adversary's reign and the establishment of God's eternal rule, where justice and righteousness prevail." Upon hearing these words, the devil's advocate fell silent, his usual retorts and cunning arguments evaporating. He felt a profound, unsettling sense of his own downfall.

Next, a great sign appeared in heaven: a woman clothed with the sun, standing on the moon, with a crown of twelve stars. She was in the throes of birth. But a great red dragon stood ready to devour her child. "This woman," explained the celestial advocate, "represents the people of God, and the dragon is the Adversary, always ready to sabotage and devour. Yet, the child, symbolizing the gospel, will be saved and ascend to God."

The devil's advocate, for the first time, felt a twinge of unease, recognizing his own likeness in the dragon. A beast rose from the sea, bearing seven heads and ten horns, with a blasphemous name on its heads. "This beast," the celestial advocate pointed out, "is symbolic of oppressive earthly powers that stand against the Most High, inspired and guided by the Adversary."

The devil's advocate felt a strange sense of pride and yet, trepidation. His influence was indeed vast, yet the narrative unfolded, inexorably leaning towards divine victory. A second beast emerged, this one from the Earth, with two horns like a lamb but speaking like a dragon. "This beast," elucidated the celestial advocate, "is an unholy prophet, leading people astray, guiding them to worship the first beast. Deception is his tool, as he mimics the holy to cloak his profanity."

The devil's advocate, witnessing this, felt a surge of defiance. "Your interpretation is presumptuous," he retorted, "the Earth-born beast is the embodiment of free will, the exercise of choice, a counterweight to divine dictation."

The Lamb and the 144,000:

Then, on Mount Zion stood the Lamb, surrounded by 144,000, having His name and His Father's name written on their foreheads. "These," the celestial advocate declared, "are the redeemed, untouched by the Adversary's deceit, committed to the Lamb. They represent the faithful remnant, those who remain steadfast despite the allure of the beasts." The devil's advocate, hearing this, felt his anger simmer. "You paint everything in stark black and white," he objected, "but life is complex, people are complex. Not all who succumb to temptation are lost."

Three angels then traversed the sky, each bearing a separate message: the eternal gospel, the fall of Babylon, and the condemnation of the beast worshipers. "These angels," said the celestial advocate, "are divine heralds, each proclaiming truth and divine judgment." The devil's advocate, unyielding, responded, "And who is to say what is the truth? Each soul should be free to discern its own truth."

As the celestial drama unfolds, the conversations between the celestial advocate and the devil's advocate intensify, each argument revealing deeper complexities of divine judgment and human will.

An image of ripe grain and grapes ready for harvest surfaced. "This," the celestial advocate noted, "symbolizes the final separation of good and evil. The faithful will be gathered and saved, while the wicked will face divine judgment."

Yet, the devil's advocate argued, "You put forward a terrifying image to enforce faith. Should belief come from fear or from love? Even in your metaphor, is it not the vine that gives life to the grape, and the earth that nourishes the grain?"

Next, seven angels appeared, each carrying a bowl filled with the wrath of God. "These angels," the celestial advocate elucidated, "will pour out the final plagues, expressing the final judgment on those who refuse God's mercy." However, the devil's advocate saw it differently.

"Mercy? It sounds more like wrath. Is this how divine love is expressed? By punishment? There should be compassion, forgiveness, and understanding."

An angel announced the fall of Babylon, symbolic of oppressive powers and decadence. "This," said the celestial advocate, "is the eventual collapse of all worldly kingdoms that disregard God's authority and mistreat His people." "Or perhaps," the devil's advocate countered, "this is the inevitable end of all hierarchies, whether they be divine or earthly. All structures eventually crumble, making way for something new."

The dialogue continued, every scene in the heavenly theater providing a new topic of debate, a new facet of truth, a new perspective on the divine narrative. Mary turned her gaze back to her guiding angel, her mind a whirlpool of thoughts, the revelations of the seals and the visions of divine justice heavy on her heart. "Will Jerusalem be destroyed?" Mary asked, her voice wavering with trepidation.

"Yes, Mary," the angel confirmed gently. "The Jerusalem of this world will face destruction. But fear not, for God has prepared a new Jerusalem, a heavenly city for Jesus and his followers."

"And James? What will become of him?" Mary asked, the fear in her heart mirrored in her eyes. The apostle James, brother of Jesus, had a special place in her heart for his kindness and his unyielding faith in the teachings of Jesus.

The angel looked at her with a mix of compassion and sorrow. "James will meet a tragic fate. His devotion to Christ and his unyielding insistence on a moral life will make him a target for religious zealots. The same hatred that led to the crucifixion of Jesus will claim his life too."

Mary gasped, her hand flying to her mouth. The death of another loved one was too much to bear. The angel, sensing her distress, sought to comfort her. "Remember, Mary, all who lose their lives for the sake of Christ will find it. James' death will be a testament to his unwavering faith, his love for Christ, and his determination to lead a moral life. His life will inspire many to turn to the teachings of Jesus, and his death will only serve to further the spread of Christianity."

"And this destruction," Mary mumbled, gathering her strength, "it is to come soon?"

"Yes, Mary. The Romans will lay siege to Jerusalem in a future not so far off. It will be a time of great unrest and turmoil, and the death of James will be a spark that ignites the population against the Sanhedrin."

"But remember, all these tribulations are part of the divine plan. Through trials and tribulations, faith is tested, and the true followers of Christ are revealed."

Mary nodded, her heart heavy with the knowledge of the trials and tribulations to come. But she also felt a strange sense of peace. In her heart, she knew that no matter what happened, God's plan was in motion. The trials of this world were but a prelude to the glory of the next.

The conversation with the angel continued, and with each revelation, Mary's faith grew stronger. The path before her and the early Christian community was fraught with danger, but their faith in Jesus and his teachings was their guiding light. For they knew that, in the end, they were heading towards the New Jerusalem, a city of light and peace, where their Savior awaited them.

Chapter 17
The Revelation of the New Jerusalem

C ertainly, here's the corrected transcription:

As their conversation moved into the later hours, the angel began to speak of a vision beyond the coming trials and tribulations. It was a vision of splendor, a place so beautiful that words could barely describe it. This was New Jerusalem, a city not built by human hands but by God Himself.

"Picture this, Mary," the angel said, his voice soft but filled with excitement. "A city of pure gold, clear as crystal. Its brilliance is like a very costly gem, like a jasper stone, clear as crystal." He gestured towards the sky, painting a vivid picture with his words. "There is a great and high wall, with twelve gates guarded by twelve angels. On these gates are written the names of the twelve tribes of the children of Israel. In the city are twelve foundations, and on them are the names of the twelve apostles of the Lamb. Each foundation is decorated with every kind of precious stone. The city has no need for the sun or the moon to shine upon it. The glory of God illuminates it, and its lamp is the Lamb. The nations will walk in its light, and the kings of the earth bring their glory into it."

The angel paused, looking at Mary. Her face was rapt with awe as she listened to the description of the city. It was beyond anything she could have imagined, a place of peace and beauty, where there would be no more sorrow, no more pain.

"In this city," the angel continued, "there will be no more death, nor sorrow, nor crying, and no more pain. The former things have passed away."

Mary let out a breath she didn't realize she was holding. The New Jerusalem seemed like a dream, a beautiful dream that stood in stark contrast to the harsh realities of the world she lived in. But it wasn't a dream. It was a promise, a promise from God Himself.

"God Himself will dwell with His people. He will wipe away every tear from their eyes, and there will be no more death, nor sorrow, nor crying, and no more pain. For the former things have passed away, and behold, He will make all things new."

The words of the angel resonated within Mary, and she clung onto them, etching them into her heart. They were a beacon of hope, a promise of a future where God's children would live in peace and love, forever in the presence of their Savior.

In this grand spiritual battle, the forces of fear and doubt often threatened to undermine the faithful. Yet, in these trials, the words of Jesus remained their refuge, "A new command I give you: Love one another. As I have loved you, so you must love one another." Even in the face of persecution and scorn, the apostles remembered these words and strove to emulate the selfless, unconditional love demonstrated by Jesus. They understood that this love was not a mere sentiment, but a force capable of transcending the barriers of prejudice, ignorance, and fear. Their actions echoed the teachings of Marcus

Aurelius, who emphasized the interconnectedness of humanity and the inherent value in serving others. He wrote, "What isn't good for the hive, isn't good for the bee." Guided by this wisdom, the apostles poured themselves into their service, spreading love as they brought the divine message to every corner of the known world.

In their mission, the apostles often met individuals burdened with guilt, shackled by past mistakes, and plagued by remorse. To them, the apostles extended the divine offer of forgiveness, a cornerstone of Jesus' teachings. It was the key to breaking free from the chains of the past, a path towards redemption and spiritual renewal. In conveying this message, they echoed the Buddha's wisdom: "Holding on to anger is like grasping a hot coal with the intent of throwing it at someone else. You are the one who gets burned." They encouraged the people to not only seek forgiveness but to extend it to others as well, promoting a cycle of reconciliation and healing.

The war between the Holy Spirit and the Adversary was not one fought with physical weapons, but with the hearts and souls of humanity at stake. It was a struggle between light and darkness, truth and deception, love and hate. The apostles, guided by the Holy Spirit, stood as vanguards of truth and love. They combated the Adversary's machinations with the divine message of Jesus, a message that echoed through the ages, promising salvation and eternal life for those who believed. In the face of the Adversary's relentless onslaught, the apostles remained unwavering. Their perseverance was a testament to their faith, a beacon of hope for all who faced spiritual trials. They were the embodiment of divine resilience, their lives a testament to the triumph of the Divine. As the echoes of this spiritual war continue to reverberate through time, the message of Jesus endures, offering a beacon of hope and salvation. And so, the apostles' legacy continues, their faith and dedication a guiding light for all who seek the path of righteousness, peace, and eternal life.

One of the letters that resonated deeply with Mary was the message to the church in Ephesus. The angel emphasized the call to remember their first love and to renew their passion for Christ. Mary pondered the significance of this message, recognizing the importance of maintaining a fervent devotion to Jesus amidst the distractions and pressures of the world. As the conversation unfolded, the angel guided Mary's understanding of the heavenly worship described in Revelation. The vivid portrayal of angels, elders, and multitudes singing praises to God captured the essence of true worship. Mary marveled at the vision, recognizing the call for believers to worship God wholeheartedly, even in the midst of adversity and persecution. The angel also drew Mary's attention to the New Jerusalem, the city described as the dwelling place of God and the redeemed. Its magnificent splendor and the absence of sorrow and pain conveyed the hope of a future where God's presence would dwell with His people. Mary's heart swelled with anticipation, longing for the day when all tears would be wiped away and true peace and joy would reign. As Mary and the angel continued their dialogue, they explored the depths of Revelation, drawing insights and understanding from the enigmatic visions. The conversation became a journey of faith, inspiring Mary to cling to the promises of God and to be a beacon of hope amidst the challenges faced by the early Christian community.

Armed with the transformative message of the Book of Revelation, Mary stepped out into the world, ready to fulfill her calling as a bearer of hope. The weight of the revelations lay heavy on her heart, but she knew that the truths contained within its pages held the power to awaken hearts and guide souls towards redemption. Her first destination was a bustling city at the crossroads of cultures and religions.

The air was thick with the scent of spices and the clamor of market activity. Here, amidst the diverse tapestry of humanity, Mary would share the revelations that had stirred her soul. As she took her place in the marketplace, a crowd began to gather around her, drawn by her presence and the air of serenity that surrounded her. With a voice filled with conviction, Mary began to speak, weaving together the insights gleaned from the Book of Revelation.

"The time is at hand," she declared, her words carrying the weight of divine truth. "The prophecies foretold in the Book of Revelation are unfolding before our very eyes. But do not despair, for in the midst of darkness, there is hope. The Lamb who was slain has conquered, and His victory is assured."

As Mary spoke, the crowd listened intently, their hearts stirred by the urgency and promise of her words. She recounted the visions of the seven seals, the trumpets, and the bowls, describing the tribulations and trials that would befall the world. "Yet, my friends," she continued, "amidst the chaos and calamity, there is a call to persevere. The book reveals that God's faithful ones will be sealed and protected, their names written in the Lamb's Book of Life. They will be guided through the darkness and emerge into the glorious light of a new creation."

Mary's words resonated deeply within the hearts of those who listened. The transformative power of Revelation gripped their souls, igniting a flicker of hope in the midst of uncertainty. As she spoke, the spiritual veil lifted, and the crowd glimpsed the eternal significance of the cosmic battle between good and evil. One by one, individuals stepped forward, their eyes filled with determination. They sought to understand more, to delve deeper into the revelations that promised both tribulation and triumph. Mary shared excerpts from the book, quoting verses that described the heavenly Jerusalem, the defeat of the dragon, and the ultimate reign of God's kingdom.

"There is a new heaven and a new earth," Mary proclaimed, her voice ringing with joy. "A place where God will wipe away every tear, where there will be no more death, mourning, crying, or pain. The former things will pass away, and all will be made new."

As the crowd dispersed, carrying the message of hope within their hearts, Mary found solace in the knowledge that the seeds of Revelation had been sown. The journey ahead was vast, and there were countless souls yearning to hear the transformative message of redemption and restoration.

Chapter 18

A Journey of Mourning and Hope

In the unseen astral realm, a discourse of great significance was taking place. The Holy Spirit and the Adversary engaged in a metaphysical dialogue, the weight of their words reverberating through the cosmos. The Holy Spirit, a radiant beacon of divine love, began, "In all beings, there is the potential for good and evil, for light and dark. This duality exists not as a curse, but as an opportunity for growth, for understanding, and for compassion.

When faced with adversity, man has the opportunity to choose love over hate, forgiveness over resentment, and integrity over deceit. This is the path of righteousness that Jesus proclaimed."

The Devil, embodiment of the seven cardinal sins, retorted, "But is it not easier to surrender to the darkness, to indulge in the pleasures of the flesh and the ego? Is it not simpler to follow the path of least resistance than to struggle against one's natural desires?"

"The path of righteousness is not easy," the Holy Spirit replied, "but it is fulfilling. Every struggle faced, every temptation resisted, brings man closer to the Divine. It offers a joy that is deeper and more enduring than the fleeting pleasures of earthly desires."

These were not mere words, but echoes of profound wisdom. The Holy Spirit's teachings mirrored those of Marcus Aurelius, who stated that "the happiness of your life depends upon the quality of your thoughts." They echoed the Dalai Lama's belief that "the purpose of our lives is to be happy," and that happiness is achieved not through material wealth, but through compassion, understanding, and peace of mind. On the other hand, the Devil's temptations bore a striking resemblance to the negative aspects of human nature.

They mirrored the cardinal sins: the allure of lust, the greed for wealth, the comfort of sloth, the satisfaction of wrath, the false confidence of pride, the insatiable nature of gluttony, and the destructive power of envy.

In Jerusalem, the apostles continued their mission, spreading the message of Jesus far and wide. They were not oblivious to the challenges they faced. They encountered skepticism, opposition, and even persecution. Yet, their resolve remained unwavering, their faith unshakable. They drew strength from the Holy Spirit, from the teachings of Jesus, and from the wisdom of great thinkers and philosophers. The apostles' journey was not just a physical one, but a spiritual one. As they walked the path of righteousness, they discovered the true meaning of happiness, joy, and an upright life. They learned that true joy does not lie in worldly pleasures, but in the love and grace of the Divine. They found that the path to an upright life lies not in following societal norms, but in acting with integrity, compassion, and love.

This dialogue of duality, between the Holy Spirit and the Adversary, between righteousness and temptation, is a reflection of the struggle within each human heart. It is a testament to the enduring power of love, the transformative potential of faith, and the promise of salvation. Meanwhile, the apostles continued their journey, their words and deeds inspiring many to turn away from their old ways and embrace the path of righteousness. As the words of Jesus spread, hearts began to change, and lives began to transform. The divine message of love, grace, and salvation, once met with skepticism and resistance, was now being embraced by more and more people. But as the light of Jesus' message grew brighter, the shadows cast by the Adversary also deepened.

The battle between love and fear, faith and doubt, salvation and sin, raged on, both in the spiritual realm and in the hearts of mankind. Yet amidst the chaos, the message of Jesus remained a beacon of hope, guiding those who were lost towards the path of righteousness. So it was that the battle continued, a timeless struggle between light and darkness. Yet, amidst the chaos and uncertainty, the message of divine love echoed, its resonance a beacon of hope and redemption. As long as hearts were willing to listen, to be transformed by love, the promise of salvation remained, a timeless beacon guiding souls towards the Divine. And so, the stage was set for the continuing struggle, an epic battle that spanned both realms, both seen and unseen.

Mary's heart was heavy with grief as she embarked on her journey to Spain. The loss of James, her beloved brother in Christ, weighed heavily on her soul. But amidst her sadness, she found solace in the presence of the angel who had been her constant companion and guide. As she traveled through the arid landscapes, her mind drifted back to the early days in Jerusalem. She marveled at how her life had been transformed by the salvation that flowed from Jesus' sacrificial love. The angel's presence, too, had been a testament to the power and reality of the spiritual realm. In a moment of quiet reflection, Mary recalled the parable shared by the angel, likening the growth of

Christianity to the life cycle of a tree. The angel had explained that just as a tree sheds its leaves in the winter, only to be reborn in the spring, so too did civilizations rise and fall, while the message of Christ endured. With this profound understanding, Mary realized that her journey to Spain held great significance. She would contribute to the growth of Christianity, even as she mourned the loss of James. The angel's interpretation of the parable had given her the strength and courage to step into the unknown and fulfill her role as a witness and recorder of the apostles' saga. As she arrived in Hispania, Mary was met with a vibrant mix of cultures and beliefs. It was a land where the Moors held sway, and the teachings of pagan gods dominated. But amidst the diversity, she sensed the longing for spiritual truth and the seeds of curiosity waiting to be nurtured. Her first encounter was with a small group of Moors, gathered under the shade of an ancient olive tree. They were captivated by her presence, drawn to the light that radiated from within her. In their midst, she shared the stories of Jesus, the miracles He performed, and the transformative power of His love. "Though I mourn the loss of my dear Jesus," Mary spoke, her voice filled with unwavering conviction, "I carry with me the hope that his sacrifice and the message he proclaimed will reach the farthest corners of the Earth. Let us embrace the unity that transcends cultural boundaries and share in the joy of salvation." Her words resonated deeply with the Moors, touching their hearts and stirring their souls. They saw in Mary a beacon of hope, a vessel through which the light of Christ shone brightly. Through her stories and personal testimonies, she kindled a curiosity and desire for a deeper understanding of the Christian faith.

Chapter 19
Triumphs in the Land of Moors

As Mary continued her journey through Hispania, she faced challenges and triumphs along the way. She encountered individuals whose lives would be forever changed by the hope she carried. Together, we witnessed the enduring power of faith and the transformative nature of God's love as it took root in the hearts of the Moors and beyond.

As Mary ventured deeper into the heartland of Spain, she encountered a land steeped in rich Moorish culture and tradition. The vibrant markets, adorned temples, and bustling cities were a testament to the power and influence of the Pagan faith. It was amidst this backdrop that Mary's journey of spreading the message of Christ continued.

Her travels took her to the great city of Cordoba, where she found herself surrounded by scholars, poets, and philosophers. The learned minds of the Pagan world engaged in fervent debates and discussions about theology, philosophy, and the nature of God. Mary saw an opportunity to engage in meaningful dialogue and share the wisdom she had gained from her experiences.

Gathered in a courtyard adorned with intricate tile work and flowing fountains, Mary engaged in spirited conversations with scholars and intellectuals. She spoke of Jesus, the Son of God, who came to bring light and salvation to all humanity. She shared the profound teachings of love, forgiveness, and compassion that Jesus had imparted to His followers.

One particular scholar, intrigued by Mary's words, challenged her with questions about the nature of God's existence and the validity of the Christian faith. Mary, guided by the angel's wisdom and the knowledge she had gained from the apostles, responded with grace and clarity. "The truth of God's existence and the validity of the Christian faith cannot be simply proven through intellectual arguments," Mary explained. "It is through the transformative power of faith, the personal encounters with Jesus Christ, and the witness of His love in our lives that we come to know the truth."

Her response sparked a flame of curiosity within the scholar, prompting him to delve deeper into the teachings of Jesus. As the days passed, Mary continued to engage in thoughtful discussions, shedding light on the Christian faith and its compatibility with the values of love, peace, and unity cherished by the Moors.

Through her interactions, Mary witnessed the remarkable transformation taking place in the hearts of the Moors. The seed of curiosity had blossomed into a genuine desire to explore the path of Christ. The angel's presence continued to guide her, providing insights and discernment in each encounter.

One evening, as Mary sought respite in the quiet solitude of a courtyard, the angel appeared before her. "Mary, your faith and unwavering commitment to sharing the message of Christ have borne fruit," the angel spoke with gentle reassurance. "In the midst of this Moorish land, the light of Christ is shining brightly. Continue to nurture the seeds of faith and watch as they grow into a magnificent garden of believers."

Overwhelmed with gratitude, Mary pondered the angel's words. She marveled at how her journey had unfolded, how she had been led from Jerusalem to the distant lands of Hispania. Though her heart still mourned the loss of James, she saw the profound purpose in her calling. She was a witness to the power of Christ's love, a conduit for His grace and truth.

Mary's journey through the land of Moors was filled with both triumphs and tribulations. As she continued to share the message of Christ, she faced resistance and opposition from those who clung tightly to their Islamic faith. The leaders of the Moorish communities saw her presence as a threat, a challenge to their authority and the established order.

Undeterred by the challenges, Mary pressed on, her heart aflame with the zeal of her mission. She sought out hidden communities of believers who practiced their faith in secret, away from the prying eyes of the ruling powers. In their company, she found solace and strength, as they shared their stories of faith and the miracles they had witnessed.

One such hidden community resided in the mountainous region of Andalusia. Nestled amidst the rugged terrain, they gathered in secret to worship and study the teachings of Jesus. Mary was welcomed with open arms, and together, they formed a bond of fellowship and resilience.

In the depths of the night, beneath a canopy of stars, Mary engaged in profound discussions with the believers. They contemplated the mysteries of faith, delving into the prophecies of the Old Testament and the revelations of Jesus. As they shared their insights, Mary marveled at the depth of their understanding and the fervor with which they embraced the Christian message.

It was during one such gathering that Mary shared the visions of John, the apostle who had witnessed the apocalyptic saga. She read aloud from her scrolls, recounting the vivid imagery of heavenly realms, angelic hosts, and the ultimate triumph of good over evil. The believers listened with bated breath, their hearts stirred with a mixture of awe and trepidation.

"These visions of John," Mary began, her voice filled with reverence, "are a testament to the eternal struggle between light and darkness, the forces of good and evil that have battled since the beginning of time. They remind us that in the midst of chaos and tribulations, God's plan of redemption and restoration will ultimately prevail."

The believers pondered her words, their faces illuminated by the flickering flames. They contemplated the significance of their own lives in the grand tapestry of God's divine plan. Mary, guided by the angel's wisdom, offered them further insights and interpretations, helping them navigate the intricate symbolism within John's visions.

As Mary's journey continued, she encountered influential leaders and scholars who held great sway over the Moorish communities. Through patient dialogue and intellectual discourse, she sought to challenge their preconceived notions and open their hearts to the possibility of a different path. Though progress was slow, she planted seeds of curiosity and doubt, knowing that God's truth would ultimately prevail.

Throughout her travels, Mary's faith was tested time and again. She faced moments of doubt and weariness, longing for the familiar streets of Jerusalem and the company of the apostles. But in those moments, the angel's presence provided solace and encouragement, reminding her of the greater purpose that fueled her journey.

As Mary embarked on her journey to the distant lands beyond Andalusia, she marveled at the diverse tapestry of ancient civilizations she encountered. The remnants of once-great empires stood as testaments to the ebb and flow of history, while vibrant cultures and traditions thrived amidst the ruins. Her path led her through the winding alleys of Cordoba, where pagan and druidic influences intertwined, creating a unique fusion of art, architecture, and knowledge.

In the temple of Cordoba, Mary stood in awe of the intricate arches and the mesmerizing play of light, a testament to the power of human creativity and devotion. From Cordoba, Mary ventured further east, traversing the arid landscapes of Al Andalus. The ancient city of Granada awaited her arrival, its majestic Alhambra Palace a symbol of beauty and resilience.

As she explored its halls adorned with intricate carvings and poetic inscriptions, Mary marveled at the rich cultural tapestry woven by the Moors. In the bustling markets of Marrakech, the vibrant colors and intoxicating aromas engulfed Mary's senses. She walked among merchants and artisans, their craftsmanship a reflection of centuries-old traditions passed down through generations. Conversations flowed freely, and in the exchanges of ideas and experiences, Mary found the universal yearning for truth and meaning.

Chapter 20
Journeys to Ancient Lands

A s her journey continued, Mary arrived at the banks of the mighty Nile River, in the land of pharaohs and pyramids. The monuments of ancient Egypt towered before her, shrouded in the mists of time. In the presence of such awe-inspiring grandeur, Mary contemplated the transient nature of human existence and the eternal power of faith that transcends earthly realms.

Traveling onward to the ancient city of Rome, Mary found herself walking amidst the remnants of an empire that ruled over vast territories. The grandeur of the Colosseum and the majesty of the Vatican stirred within her a deep sense of awe and reverence. She visited the catacombs, where Peter and the early Christians sought refuge and worshiped in secret, their faith unyielding even in the face of persecution. Amidst these encounters with ancient lands and civilizations, Mary's heart remained steadfast in its devotion to the teachings of Jesus. She drew strength from the memories of His ministry, the miracles witnessed, and the profound love He embodied. The angel by her side offered guidance and solace, reminding her of the importance of her role in spreading the message of salvation.

As Mary reflected on her journey, she marveled at the interconnectedness of humanity's quest for meaning and purpose. From the rolling hills of Galilee to the distant lands she now traversed, the yearning for truth and the search for redemption knew no boundaries. She realized that her presence in these ancient lands was not a coincidence but part of a divine plan to touch lives and illuminate hearts.

As Her Episode progresses, join us as Mary's path takes her to new frontiers, where she encounters vibrant cultures, ancient wisdom, and the enduring power of faith. Together, we will witness the transformative journey of a woman called to bear witness to the message of Jesus Christ and leave an indelible mark on the world.

As Mary embarked on her journey to the distant lands of Gaul and Britannia, she carried within her a sacred purpose: to continue the work of Jesus' ministry and spread the message of salvation. Her path led her through picturesque landscapes, where the whispers of history intertwined with the mysteries of faith.

In the enchanting city of Paris, Mary was captivated by the elegance. Amidst the vibrant streets and bustling cafes, Mary felt the presence of ancient wisdom echoing through the centuries. From Paris, Mary ventured into the verdant countryside of Gaul. She traveled along the pilgrimage routes, following in the footsteps of countless believers who sought solace and enlightenment. In the tranquil beauty of the countryside, she encountered humble chapels and monastic communities, havens of prayer and contemplation.

As she crossed the English Channel, Mary arrived in Britannia, a land steeped in Celtic traditions and Roman influence. The ancient stone circles of Stonehenge stood as enigmatic guardians of an ancient past. In the mystical landscapes of Avalon, Mary found herself drawn to the legends of Celtic superstitions, intertwining with the profound spiritual significance of her own journey.

Returning to Gaul, Mary felt a calling deep within her soul. In the picturesque region of Provence, amidst the rugged beauty of the landscape, she established a monastery, a sanctuary of devotion and learning. Here, the teachings of Jesus would be preserved and nurtured, serving as a beacon of hope in a world filled with uncertainty and darkness. The monastery became a gathering place for seekers of truth, scholars, and those who sought solace in their faith. Mary's presence radiated compassion and wisdom, drawing pilgrims from far and wide. Within the hallowed halls, knowledge was preserved, illuminated manuscripts were crafted, and discussions on theology and philosophy flourished.

Through her unwavering commitment to the ministry of Jesus, Mary became a guiding light in the advancement of Christianity. Her journey, from the humble streets of Jerusalem to the sacred lands of Gaul and Britannia, was guided by a divine plan, a plan shrouded in mystery and revealed in unexpected ways. This mysterious journey, a tapestry of ancient lands and profound spiritual encounters, served as the inspiration for a continuation of Mary's quest to protect the sacred truths she carried. In the footsteps of the Apostles, delve into the depths of Mary's knowledge and the hidden wisdom she possessed.

Chapter 21
Simon Peter's Vision

Mary, my dear companion and faithful recorder of our adventures, resided in Jerusalem. She diligently chronicled the events that unfolded, relaying my trials and triumphs to our congregations. We often discussed the significance of what I was establishing, realizing that the foundation I was laying would become the rock Jesus had prophesied about.

From the moment Jesus found and called me to be his disciple, my life changed forever. I was Simon, a simple fisherman, but Jesus saw something in me that I had never seen in myself. He gave me a new name, Peter, declaring that I would be the rock upon which he would build his church. With a mixture of awe and trepidation, I followed him throughout his ministry, witnessing miracles, listening to his teachings, and basking in his divine presence. But nothing could have prepared me for the sorrow of witnessing his crucifixion. My heart shattered as I watched my beloved teacher and friend suffer on that cross. However, my despair turned to awe and elation when I witnessed his resurrection and ascension. Jesus had triumphed over death, and his mission was now entrusted to us, his disciples. Filled with the

Holy Spirit, I embarked on a journey across lands and seas, spreading the message of Jesus' love and salvation.

In Greece, I found eager believers and engaged in spirited debates with Greek philosophers, sharing the wisdom of Jesus and challenging their cherished beliefs. My words stirred hearts and ignited a fire of faith, but they also drew the ire of religious leaders, fueled by whispers from the devil. As the threats against me grew, I knew it was time to move on. My journey led me to the great city of Rome, the heart of the mighty empire. Through divine providence, I was introduced to a wealthy family with influence and power. They became my protectors and supporters, and through their conversion, they established a shield around me as I navigated the dangerous waters of Rome's political and religious landscape.

But the devil, ever cunning, conspired against me. Despite the family's protection, I was arrested and brought before the Roman authorities on charges of sedition and heresy. The trials were a farce, orchestrated by those threatened by the growing influence of the Christian message. Yet, even in the face of persecution, my faith remained unyielding.

In the depths of my grief, I had a vision. I saw Christianity taking root in Rome, spreading like wildfire through the hearts of its people. I foresaw a future where the religion of Rome would be transformed, where its emperors would embrace the faith. And indeed, it would come to pass centuries later when Constantine, the Eastern Roman Emperor, converted to Christianity after a vision of victory under the banner of the Christian cross. As I witnessed the trial and crucifixion of my dear brother Peter, a profound sadness washed over me. But instead of withering like a fragile flower, my faith grew stronger. I knew that Peter's sacrifice and the foundation he laid in Rome would become the cornerstone of the Church, influencing not only the

Western and Eastern Roman Empires but also reaching far beyond, across Europe and to the Britannia Isles. Through tears that stained the parchment, I recorded the saga of Peter's journey and the growth of Christianity in Rome.

The angel by my side enveloped my spirit with a shield of joy, and the devil seethed with anger. I remained steadfast, knowing that this faith, this message of salvation, would prevail and change the course of history. As I continued my own journey, navigating the tumultuous currents of Jerusalem, I couldn't help but feel the weight of Peter's absence. He had been a pillar of strength, an unwavering source of guidance and inspiration. Now, his martyrdom served as a somber reminder of the sacrifices we were called to make in spreading the gospel. In the midst of my grief, the devil seized upon the opportunity to sow seeds of doubt and despair. He whispered insidious lies, questioning the validity of our mission and tempting me to abandon my post. But I clung to the words of Jesus, the memories of his teachings that resounded within my heart. I knew that our purpose was greater than any earthly tribulation. With renewed resolve, I focused on continuing Peter's work.

The vibrant congregation we had built in Jerusalem rallied together, their faith unshaken by the tragedy we had endured. Together, we carried the torch of truth, steadfast in our commitment to sharing the transformative message of Jesus. But the road ahead was treacherous. The religious leaders, threatened by our growing influence, intensified their efforts to suppress our movement. They launched persecutions, unleashing their fury upon the followers of Christ. Many faced imprisonment, torture, and even death for their unwavering faith. In the face of such adversity, we were forced to go into hiding, seeking shelter in secret locations known only to a select few. Our gatherings became clandestine, hidden from prying eyes. Yet, even in the shadows, our numbers continued to grow. The devil's attempts to extinguish the flame of Christianity only fueled its spread. As I wrote the saga of our struggles and triumphs, I couldn't help but marvel at the power of faith. The words flowed from my pen, guided by the Holy Spirit, weaving a tapestry of courage and resilience.

Each chapter chronicled the stories of men and women who defied persecution, who stood firm in their conviction, and who were willing to sacrifice everything for the sake of the gospel. In the darkest of times, I drew strength from the visions I had seen. I saw the eventual triumph of Christianity, its message echoing across time and space. I saw emperors and kings kneeling before the cross, their hearts transformed by the love of Christ. I saw nations embracing the teachings of Jesus, and a new era of hope dawning upon the world. The devil's fury only served to fortify my resolve. I knew that as long as there were souls in need of salvation, as long as there was darkness to be dispelled, our mission would endure. Peter's sacrifice had ignited a flame that would burn bright through the ages, guiding lost souls toward the path of redemption. And so, with pen in hand and a heart filled with determination, I continued to record the epic tale of our struggles and triumphs. Each chapter was a testament to the indomitable spirit of the early Christians, to their unwavering faith in the face of persecution. Through their stories, I hoped to inspire future generations, to remind them of the price that had been paid for the freedom to believe. As I penned the final words of each chapter, I couldn't help but but marvel at the power of faith. The words flowed from my pen, guided by the Holy Spirit, weaving a tapestry of courage and resilience. Each chapter chronicled the stories of men and women who defied persecution, who stood firm in their conviction, and who were willing to sacrifice everything for the sake of the gospel. In the darkest of times, I drew strength from the visions I had seen. I saw the eventual triumph of Christianity, its message echoing across time and space. I saw emperors and kings kneeling before the cross, their hearts transformed by the love of Christ. I saw nations embracing the teachings of Jesus, and a new era of hope dawning upon the world.

The devil's fury only served to fortify my resolve. I knew that as long as there were souls in need of salvation, as long as there was darkness to be dispelled, our mission would endure. Peter's sacrifice had ignited a flame that would burn bright through the ages, guiding lost souls toward the path of redemption. And so, with pen in hand and a heart filled with determination, I continued to record the epic tale of our struggles and triumphs. Each chapter was a testament to the indomitable spirit of the early Christians, to their unwavering faith in the face of persecution. Through their stories, I hoped to inspire future generations, to remind them of the price that had been paid for the freedom to believe. As I penned the final words of each chapter, I couldn't help but wonder what lay ahead for us, for the infant Church that was taking its first steps into a hostile world. But one thing remained certain: the light of Christ would never be extinguished. It would continue to shine, illuminating the hearts of those who sought truth, guiding them home to the embrace of a loving Savior.

Chapter 22
The Tainted Heart

The spiritual realm was a canvas of swirling energies, a backdrop against which the grand struggle for souls unfolded. The Holy Spirit and the Devil, as old as Creation itself, were entangled in a cosmic dance. Each step, each pirouette, each grand leap represented an action in the material world, shaping the course of human existence.

In this spectral dance, the Holy Spirit, drawn from the wisdom of sages and prophets, embodied love, mercy, forgiveness, and joy. It was a beacon of serenity amidst the tumult, a lighthouse guiding lost ships through stormy seas. The teachings of Christ—"love your neighbor as yourself," "turn the other cheek," "the meek shall inherit the Earth"—became the rhythm to which it swayed.

The Devil, on the other hand, danced to the beat of discord, sowing seeds of doubt, fear, and confusion in the minds of those whose faith was newly kindled. It reveled in earthly desires, fueled by the writings of men who championed power, ambition, and self-indulgence. From the tales of greed in Rome to the teachings of philosophers who promoted material wealth and physical pleasure, the Devil skillfully utilized these ideas to influence mankind towards earthly distraction.

For every soul that the apostles saved, the Adversary sought to taint. It whispered into the ears of kings, priests, and the rich, stoking their fear of losing power and influence. The devilish symphony it conducted played on the heartstrings of the vulnerable, causing them to waver in their newfound faith. Yet, for all the chaos and discord it wove, the Devil found its efforts often thwarted. For every seed of doubt it planted, the Holy Spirit was there to nurture faith. For every fear it instilled, the Holy Spirit reminded the faithful of God's everlasting love and protection. For every soul it swayed towards darkness, the Holy Spirit was there to light the way back.

And so, the grand dance of Eternity continued, the spiritual realm echoing the melodies of this cosmic ballet. The outcome, uncertain and unpredictable, was in the hands of each individual soul. Free will was the wild card, the unpredictable element that could tip the scales in either direction. Amid this epic struggle, the apostles continued their mission, guided by the Holy Spirit. They faced persecution, pain, and death with courage and unwavering faith, becoming beacons of hope and love amidst the darkness. The Holy Spirit whispered into their hearts, reminding them of Christ's teachings: "Blessed are those who are persecuted because of righteousness, for theirs is the kingdom of heaven." Their actions, their sacrifices, and their unwavering faith were testament to the enduring power of love and kindness, lighting the path for others to follow.

For the faithful, each day was a dance with Eternity, a step in the grand ballet that echoed through the spiritual realm. And with each step, with each pirouette, with each grand leap, they had a choice. A choice to embrace love, to cultivate kindness, to foster forgiveness, or to succumb to the whispers of the Adversary. The dance continues, the music of the cosmic ballet playing on, and the souls of mankind continue to sway in the grand dance of Eternity.

In the metaphysical plane, an ethereal realm stretched beyond the grasp of ordinary human perception, two monumental figures held a dialogue. Their words weren't spoken but exchanged as profound thought, interweaving wisdom, spirituality, and ethics.

"I bring the eternal message of the enlightened one," the first figure stated, a luminescent embodiment of divine warmth and compassion, "A discourse of peace, love, and interconnectedness. His teachings resonate with the deepest truth of existence and are a guide to transcending the cycle of suffering, awakening to the reality of the impermanence of all things." The figure's words echoed the teachings of Jesus, a deep understanding of suffering and the path to its cessation. It represented the Holy Spirit's mission to enlighten the hearts of humanity, unveiling the path to salvation that lay in the teachings of Christ.

A contrasting figure, enveloped in dark energy, responded, "I have been tasked to test the fortitude of beings. To present them with temptations and desires, the seven cardinal sins. I am the architect of obstacles, an advocate for the ego, and the material. My role is not to encourage evil but to highlight the power of choice and the consequences it brings." His words represented the Devil's advocacy. It is in overcoming his tests that individuals demonstrate the strength of their character and their commitment to their path.

Marcus Aurelius once stated, "You have power over your mind, not outside events. Realize this, and you will find strength." These words found resonance in the Holy Spirit's discourse, emphasizing the importance of inner resilience and wisdom in overcoming external temptations and difficulties.

"The enlightened one's teachings hold a similar message," the Holy Spirit replied. "Inner peace, clarity, and wisdom can overcome the cycle of desire and suffering. The path to salvation that Jesus showed is a testament to this universal truth. His message of love, forgiveness, and selflessness is the antidote to the illusions you create."

Jesus' teachings on compassion, ethics, and happiness were also reflected in the Holy Spirit's dialogue. It emphasized that leading a life guided by love, kindness, and integrity was key to achieving enduring joy and peace, the essence of Jesus' message.

The Devil, unmoved, retorted, "I represent a vital component of existence. Without darkness, how can one appreciate the light? Without trials, how does one realize their strength? The seven cardinal sins are not evils but challenges to be overcome."

In this exchange, the Holy Spirit and the Devil delved deep into their roles in the cosmic drama. Each had their part to play in the grand scheme of things—one as the beacon of salvation, and the other as the tester of virtues. Their dialogues continued, weaving profound philosophy and spiritual wisdom, shaping the course of human history. This was their eternal dance, an epic struggle between light and darkness, played out across the ages in the hearts and minds of mankind.

The Holy Spirit, seeing the difficulty in her mission to spread the teachings of Christ far and wide, called upon the wisdom of various enlightened beings, seeking guidance on how to establish a network, an infrastructure that could disseminate Jesus' message without it being diluted or altered by existing pagan beliefs. Drawing inspiration from the orderliness and discipline of the Roman centurion ranks, she envisioned a similar structure for the Church, a hierarchy tempered by Christian ethics of peace, love, and harmony. Bishops, priests, deacons—each with their roles and responsibilities, all working together for a common cause—to spread the gospel of Jesus Christ.

The Holy Spirit recognized that, like the martyrdom of the Apostles, the establishment and growth of this new Christian faith would be her legacy. She realized that just as the Apostles had built the faith of

Christianity through their sacrifices, her work would lay the groundwork for a spiritual institution that would endure through the ages, saving countless souls.

Meanwhile, the Devil, threatened by the spread of this 'spiritual virus,' plotted to hinder the rise of Christianity. He used his influence over human desires, fears, and uncertainties to undermine the new faith. He knew well that change was intimidating and that humans would cling to their familiar beliefs out of fear of the unknown.

Despite his efforts, the Holy Spirit remained resolute, remembering the teachings of Christ, "In this world, you will have trouble. But take heart! I have overcome the world." She knew she had to fortify the resolve of the believers against the onslaught of the Devil's temptations.

The Holy Spirit's strategy was simple but profound: to promote the embodiment of Christ's teachings of love, compassion, forgiveness, and self-sacrifice. For she knew that the message of salvation through Christ was the answer to mankind's eternal search for happiness, joy, and a purposeful life.

Thus, a timeless conflict ensued. The Holy Spirit, steadfast in her mission, built churches and faith communities across various lands, inspiring leaders, and guiding believers. The Devil, in his obstinacy, continued to weave webs of deceit and temptation, exploiting human frailties. Despite his relentless efforts, the Holy Spirit's influence continued to grow. Churches rose in Britannia, Gaul, Scotland, Germania, Portugal, and Hispania, becoming bastions of faith, preserving the teachings of Christ, and guiding souls towards salvation.

Through centuries of trials and tribulations, victories and defeats, the Holy Spirit and the Devil played their parts in this epic drama of humanity's spiritual journey. Yet, in the end, the strength of the message of Jesus—of unconditional love, forgiveness, and the pursuit of righteousness—would stand against the test of time, providing hope and guidance for billions of souls through the ages.

As the Christian faith flourished and grew, there emerged the need for individuals to lead and serve the burgeoning congregations. The Holy Spirit, guiding the hearts of the faithful, bestowed gifts of leadership, wisdom, and service. These individuals, in the name of Christ and with the strength of their conviction, became the hands, feet, and voice of Jesus on Earth.

However, this was not without its challenges. The Devil saw these leaders as threats to his dominion, and he aimed his arrows of temptation, doubt, and deception at them. Yet the Holy Spirit would not abandon those chosen for this sacred duty. She equipped them with armor of faith, shields of righteousness, and swords of truth to stand against the Devil's schemes.

The infrastructure that the Holy Spirit had envisioned began to take shape. From the local parish priests to bishops overseeing vast regions, each played a critical role in maintaining the integrity of the Gospel message as it was disseminated across diverse cultures and lands.

The faith that started as a small spark in Jerusalem ignited into a flame that spread across the world. The teachings of Christ, embedded in love, compassion, and salvation, transcended cultural barriers, touching the hearts of people from all walks of life.

The struggle between the Holy Spirit and the Devil was not a battle won in a day, nor was it one that would end. It was, and continues to be, a spiritual warfare that spans millennia. Yet, amidst this eternal struggle, the Holy Spirit's legacy persisted. She inspired countless men and women to carry the torch of faith, ensuring that the light of Christ would never be extinguished.

The infrastructure she helped establish—the Church—became a vessel for the word of Christ, guiding countless souls towards salvation, giving hope in despair, love in hate, and peace in chaos. And so, the saga continues, the timeless battle between good and evil, between love and hate, between Christ and the Devil. The Holy Spirit, through her guidance, perseverance, and love, ensures that the teachings of Christ continue to be a beacon of hope, a light that shines in the darkness, a message of love that transcends time, guiding billions of souls towards salvation.

In this epic struggle, there came times of testing for both the Church and individuals within it. Faced with persecution, conflict, and doubt, they were compelled to look within, to question and affirm their commitment to the teachings of Christ. The Devil, ever the deceiver, sought to use these moments of uncertainty to sow discord and weaken the faithful. But through these trials, the Holy Spirit was present. She offered comfort in the midst of sorrow, wisdom amidst confusion, and courage against fear.

The words of Jesus, preserved and shared through the Church, provided a steady anchor, reminding all of God's unfailing love and the promise of salvation. As the Church expanded across continents, the apostles played a pivotal role in shaping its teachings and traditions. Their words and actions, chronicled in the Gospels and other Christian writings, served as a guide for believers across generations. Despite the Devil's attempts to distort the apostles' messages, the Holy Spirit ensured that their wisdom and teachings remained pure, leading individuals to recognize and rebuke falsehoods that were contrary to Christ's teachings.

The apostles' influence continued to echo through time, reminding believers of the core tenets of their faith and offering guidance amidst the changing tides of the world.

Chapter 23
The Timeless Promise

Over centuries, the Holy Spirit has continued to uphold the promise made to Mary: to preserve and guide the Christian faith through an ever changing world. Despite challenges, the Church has endured, providing a spiritual home for billions and serving as a beacon of hope, love, and salvation. The Devil, still seeking to sow chaos and despair, continues his machinations. Yet, he is constantly met with the light of Christ, carried by those who walk in love, stand in truth, and abide in the hope of the Gospel. As this timeless saga unfolds, it bears witness to the enduring power of faith, the strength of the human spirit, and the eternal promise of divine love. The Holy Spirit, ever present, continues to inspire, guide, and nurture believers, sustaining the Church and affirming the promise of salvation for all who believe.

The legacy of this journey is a testament to the transformative power of Christ's teachings, a light that will continue to shine, guiding countless souls to salvation across the annals of time.Just as Mary, the mother of Jesus, had once held the Son of God in her arms, so now Mary Magdalene found herself as the caregiver of a burgeoning movement that would reshape the course of human history. She, too, understood her role with profound humility; her task was unique and essential. As Jesus had once needed a mother in his formative years, so too did this new embodiment of His divine presence on Earth, His Church, require a guiding figure. Mary Magdalene was chosen to serve as this guardian spirit, to protect and nurture the Church in its spiritual infancy

Laying the Foundations

The angel had declared that Mary Magdalene would not stand alone in this sacred duty. There would rise leaders, apostles, and saints to stand with her in the construction of the Church's edifice, and in the creation of sanctuaries for the faithful. These would be places where followers of Christ could retreat from worldly concerns to devote themselves to spiritual growth and the propagation of Jesus's teachings. With unwavering commitment, Mary Magdalene labored to turn these visions into reality. She collaborated with the Apostles, sought advice from early Christian leaders, and devoted countless hours to prayer and contemplation, requesting divine guidance in every decision she made.

Under Mary Magdalene's tender care, the Church flourished. It expanded not just in size but also in spirit and truth, emulating Christ's teachings and providing a beacon of hope amid life's turmoil. It brought Mary Magdalene immense comfort to witness the fruits of her relentless dedication, to see the Church standing as a sanctuary for the faithful, and a platform from which Christ's teachings continued to touch and transform souls. The Mission of the Church However, the Church's journey was not without hurdles. There were those who aimed to distort Christ's teachings, and others who desired to exploit the Church for personal gain. Part of Mary Magdalene's mission was to shield the Church from such threats. She became a guardian of the Church's integrity, ensuring that its followers' faith remained pure and that the holy message of Christ stayed unadulterated in the hearts of believers. As her life progressed, Mary Magdalene found solace in the knowledge that the Church she had nurtured was fulfilling its divine purpose, spreading the message of salvation and offering comfort, guidance, and love to those in search. As the spiritual mother of the Church, her legacy was one of selfless devotion, enduring love, and unwavering faith, inspiring countless generations that followed.

Mary Magdalene embarked on a journey beyond the lands she knew. The calling of the Holy Spirit led her west, to Gaul. The travel was arduous and fraught with perils, yet she found strength in prayer and contemplation, placing her trust in God's divine guidance. Upon reaching Gaul, she found fertile ground for Jesus's teachings. She immediately set to work on her divine mission, establishing the first monastery to serve as a bastion of Christ's message. This sacred place was intended to be a sanctuary of devotion, where followers of Christ could deepen their faith and expand their understanding of the Gospel. The Vision for Britannia and the Northern Highlands But her vision was not limited to Gaul. Her sights were set on the island nation of Britannia and the Northern Highlands of the Scots. She harbored hope that the word of Jesus would penetrate the heart of these lands, dispelling the shadow of pagan rituals and idolatry, and replacing them with the light of Christ's love and wisdom.

The Quest for Londinium ,With a faith as solid as a rock, Mary Magdalene directed her steps towards Londinium, the heart of Britannia. She knew the importance of establishing the presence of the Church in this vibrant city, a hub of commerce and politics. Her prayer was to find a suitable location for the Church, a place that would welcome all seekers of truth, and where the Lord's work could be done in peace and harmony. The Meeting with Quintus A key figure in her journey in Britannia was the Roman garrison commander, Quintus. She knew the Roman's garrison commander had a reputation for being a tough, pragmatic man, unyielding to new ideas. Yet, she also knew that God often worked in the most unlikely places and through the most unexpected people. She prayed that Quintus would be open to the Gospel's message, and that his heart might be touched by the profound love and peace that Jesus offered. The most considerable obstacle she anticipated was the entrenched belief in the pagan gods of the Druids and the idolatry of the Romans. They had long been part of the culture and tradition of these lands, and introducing a new spiritual perspective was a daunting task. But Mary Magdalene held an unwavering belief in the transformative power of Christ's teachings. She was prepared to demonstrate, with love and patience, that the path to true peace, joy, and salvation lay in embracing the word of Jesus. In the face of these challenges, she held tightly to her faith, ready to sow the seeds of a new spiritual awakening. It was her hope that these lands, too, would experience the transformative power of Christ's love, and embrace the salvation that His teachings offered.

The angel's voice echoed gently in the silent night, filling Mary's heart with tranquility. His words painted a vivid image of the future, a destiny of triumph and heartache intermingled. "Mary, you have been chosen to shepherd the budding faith of Christ," the angel began, his voice steady and reassuring. "The apostles are the seeds, sowing the message of Jesus in the hearts of people across the world. But a seed requires a gardener, someone to tend and protect it, to guide its growth. This will be your calling." He painted for her a vision of Europe, a continent divided by language, culture, and faith, yet bound together by an invisible thread of yearning. From the rugged high-lands of Britannia to the sun kissed shores of Hispania, from the vast plains of Germania to the fertile vineyards of Gaul, she saw the people warriors and farmers, nobles and slaves, all longing for salvation, for something greater than themselves. Her heart was heavy at the sight, for she knew the trials they would face.

The apostles' message was revolutionary, and the old powers would not surrender their influence without a fight. But amidst the turmoil, she also saw hope. She saw the ember of faith in the eyes of the faithful, ready to burst into flame with just a spark. "It will not be easy, Mary," the angel continued. "The apostles will face resistance, and many will pay the ultimate price for their faith. But their sacrifices will not be in vain. They will lay the foundation for a faith that will endure through the centuries, spreading across continents, touching billions of lives. And you, Mary, will be the architect of this great endeavor."

Mary's mind spun with questions, fears, and doubts, but in the depth of her heart, she found an unwavering resolve. She was not a warrior or a scholar, but she was a believer. And her faith, she knew, was her greatest weapon.

"I will do what is required of me," she said, her voice steady and resolute. "For the love of Christ and his teachings, I will build this foundation." And thus, Mary embarked on her journey, not as a passive observer, but as an active participant in shaping the future of Christianity. The apostles, with their unshakeable faith and martyrdom, would inspire belief, and she, with her wisdom and dedication, would build the framework that would sustain this burgeoning faith, guiding it to become a beacon of hope, love, and salvation for generations to come. As Mary awakened from the divine vision, a surge of determination coursed through her. She carried an invisible yet tangible mantle of responsibility, bestowed upon her by God's divine design. "First, you will need to understand the people, their languages, their cultures, and their hearts," the angel advised, his voice calm and steady. "You will not be alone in this task. God will guide your path, and you will encounter allies along the way. Individuals filled with the spirit of Christ, ready to heed the call."

Mary journeyed to the lands of Britannia, Gaul, Germania, Hispania, and Portugal, each land presenting its unique challenges and opportunities. Yet, in each place, she found common threads of human longing: the desire for peace, love, hope, and understanding. In Britannia, she encountered the Celts, a people proud of their traditions and wary of outsiders. Yet their druidic beliefs, steeped in respect for the natural world and the spirit that pervades it, offered fertile soil for the seeds of Christ's message. It was there she found Patrick, a young man of faith who had a vision of bringing the teachings of Christ to his people. With him, she built the first outposts of Christian faith.

In Hispania, the Roman influence was strong, and the existing pantheon of gods deeply ingrained. Yet, there was also a growing disenchantment with the old ways, a yearning for a faith that spoke to the heart, not just the mind. She found her ally in James the Greater, one of Jesus' own apostles, who had journeyed far from his homeland to preach the good news. Together, they built churches and established congregations that would withstand the test of time. With every step, Mary was the invisible hand guiding the development of the faith. She was the one who picked up the pieces when things fell apart, the one who whispered words of encouragement when spirits faltered, the one who kept the flame of faith alive even in the darkest of times. Through trials and tribulations, Mary carried the burden of her divine mission, never faltering in her resolve. "God has granted us the ability to spread the Word," Mary would tell her fellow disciples, "We must trust in His divine plan, and our faith must be unshakeable. For it is not in the ease of acceptance, but in the face of adversity that our faith is truly tested and purified." And so, in the years to follow, Mary continued her work. She built the foundational structure that allowed Christianity to spread and flourish. She encountered many who would become saints, scholars, and servants of the faith, each playing their part in the divine tapestry.

And though the world remained fraught with resistance, the message of Jesus continued to spread, reaching the hearts and souls of millions across the world. Mary's mission was bearing fruit, and she knew, even in the face of relentless opposition, their faith was building something that would echo through the ages. As Mary continued her travels, she became increasingly aware of the need for a solid, united structure to guide the burgeoning faith. Drawing inspiration from the organization of the Roman army, she saw the potential in a hierarchical system. However, the militaristic domination and exploitation of the Romans were far from the Christian ideals. Instead, she envisioned a structure based on service, humility, and guidance where each level was responsible for the spiritual well being of those under their care. In Britannia, she worked with Patrick to establish the foundational roles within their churches. They created the position of the Deacon, a servant of the church tasked with attending to the needs of the congregation. Above them were the Priests, dedicated men who conducted the services and provided spiritual guidance to the flock, At the top were the Bishops, individuals with a deep understanding and commitment to the faith. They were responsible for several churches, ensuring consistency in teaching and practice across their diocese. Lastly, the Archbishops and Cardinals oversaw large regions, ensuring unity of faith across vast territories.

In Hispania, with James the Greater, they continued to refine this structure. Recognizing the need for a central figure to guide the universal Church, they instituted the role of the Pope. This role was not one of domination, but of servitude and stewardship. The Pope was to be the servant of the servants of God, guiding the church on the path of love, mercy, and righteousness as per Jesus' teachings. To further ensure that the word of Christ was not diluted or corrupted, Mary emphasized the importance of councils, gatherings of Bishops, and Archbishops to discuss and decide on matters of faith and doctrine. These councils drew upon the wisdom of many, fostering a spirit of collective discernment rather than autocratic rule. In each land, the structure was replicated, adjusted slightly to cater to the cultural differences but always maintaining the core principles of service and humility. The model was effective. It allowed the church to grow and spread without losing its essence. It offered believers a sense of belonging and guidance, a beacon in their quest for spiritual growth. Mary's journey was long and arduous, but her faith never wavered. She knew that her work was of divine importance. The structure she was building would allow Christianity to endure through centuries, preserving the teachings of Jesus and offering spiritual refuge to billions. Even as the political landscape around them shifted, as kingdoms rose and fell, the Church remained. It was a testament to the resilience of faith, the strength of a unified belief system, and the tireless efforts of a woman guided by a vision. Mary, through her service and dedication, was indeed laying the foundation of an institution that would stand the test of time.

Chapter 24
I -The Devil

A s the apostles continued their missions, I, the Devil, observed their every move with a mix of disdain and determination. Mary Magdalene, unaware of my presence, diligently chronicled their exploits, unknowingly becoming a vessel for the spread of their message. While the apostles embraced their divine calling, I weaved my web of temptation, seeking to corrupt their hearts and twist their intentions. In the shadows, I whispered doubts, insecurities, and ambitions, hoping to exploit their human vulnerabilities. Thomas, known for his skepticism, ventured into distant lands, spreading the Gospel with unwavering determination. I preyed upon his doubts, fueling the fire of disbelief that lingered within him. With each encounter, I planted seeds of uncertainty, encouraging him to question the very foundations of his faith. James, the brother of Jesus, found himself thrust into a position of leadership within the early Christian community. I sought to exploit his familiarity with power and influence, enticing him with visions of grandeur and control. Slowly but surely, I tugged at the strings of his ambition, manipulating him into pursuing his own agenda rather than embracing the selflessness of Christ's teachings. As Mary Magdalene documented their journeys, I reveled in the battles raging within their hearts. I planted whispers of resentment, envy, and pride, exploiting their human weaknesses to lead them astray. Each apostle faced their own personal demons, unknowingly dancing on the precipice of moral compromise. The divine mission was not without its challenges. The apostles encountered resistance, skepticism, and persecution. Yet, it was the internal struggles that posed the greatest threat to their purpose. I seized upon these moments of weakness, infiltrating their thoughts and emotions with my poisonous influence. In her earnestness to capture the truth, Mary Magdalene remained a beacon of light amidst the encroaching darkness. Little did she know that my minions were listening, watching, seeking any opportunity to hinder her work and undermine the apostles' efforts. As the story unfolded, the stage was set for a grand showdown between light and darkness. The apostles, unknowingly caught in my snare, would face their greatest tests yet. The battles they waged would not only be against external forces but also the shadows within their own souls.

In My opposition to this movement, we shall delve deeper into the internal struggles of the apostles and witness the extent of my malevolent influence. The clash between light and darkness would reach a crescendo, leaving their faith and resolve hanging in the balance. But I, the Devil, saw an opportunity in Peter's unwavering faith. I whispered doubts in his ear, planting seeds of pride and arrogance. I enticed him with visions of grandeur and authority, appealing to his human weaknesses. As Peter's ministry expanded to the city of Rome, I set the stage for a confrontation that would test the very foundation of his faith. A pretender emerged, claiming to perform miracles in the name of God. The impostor sought to deceive the masses and undermine Peter's authority. But Peter, guided by the Holy Spirit, saw through the charade. He confronted the pretender in a public spectacle, invoking the power of God to expose the truth. The impostor's illusions crumbled, revealing him as a mere vessel of deceit. The people, witnessing the true power of God in Peter's words and actions, reaffirmed their faith and turned away from the imposter. It was a triumphant moment, a testament to Peter's unyielding commitment to the truth and the unwavering faith of the believers.

However, the religious leaders, threatened by Peter's influence, continued to conspire against him. They spread rumors and false accusations, seeking to discredit his mission and turn the people against him. But Peter, rooted in the divine power that flowed through him, remained steadfast in his resolve. Each day brought new challenges and triumphs as Peter's hands became instruments of God's mercy. The blind received sight, the lame found strength to walk, and the broken hearted experienced profound healing. These miracles served as a beacon of hope, igniting a spark of faith within the hearts of all who witnessed them. But I, the Devil, persisted in my efforts to undermine Peter's faith. I continued to sow seeds of doubt and temptation, preying on his vulnerabilities. I knew that if I could corrupt his unwavering commitment, the foundation of the Christian movement would be shaken. Yet, Peter's faith stood firm. He drew strength from his encounters with Jesus, from the teachings and miracles he had witnessed firsthand. His humility, once tested, grew stronger in the face of adversity. The battle between good and evil raged on, but Peter, guided by the Holy Spirit, remained a pillar of faith. His journey was marked by trials and triumphs, but through it all, he clung to the hope and redemption offered by the message of Jesus. As the chapters of Peter's saga unfolded, his influence spread far and wide, shaping the course of Christianity for generations to come. The Devil's attempts to break his faith only served to strengthen it, for Peter had experienced the power and love of God in ways that could never be shaken. And so, the story continued, with Peter as a steadfast beacon of light in a world fraught with darkness. The trials he faced only fueled his determination to spread the message of salvation and to bring hope to a world in need.

Simon Peter, the one proclaimed by Jesus to be the rock of the church,the body of Christ in the fledgling Religion of Christianity, stepped forward with an air of divine confidence. His words, dripping with conviction,touched the masses. He preached of promises and miracles, luring them deeper into the web of his divine saga. Little did they know that their newfound faith would be their salvation. While the apostles reveled in their Sagas of Jesus' Message, I watched from afar, weaving my own intricate web of corruption. My minions whispered poison into the ears of the religious and political leaders, stoking their fears and doubts. They would become the unwitting instruments of my malevolence, working to undermine the apostles' message at every turn. Their opportunity came when Peter was arrest-ed and thrown into jail. They hoped that confinement would break his spirit and silence his message. But they underestimated the power of his unwavering faith. Even behind bars, Peter continued to convert souls to Jesus. He knew his trial would be a spectacle, an opportunity to reach the multitudes of lost sinners in Rome. As the day of his trial arrived, Peter stood resolute. The Holy Spirit infused him with words of great power, touching the hearts of anyone who listened. But the hearts of the religious leaders and politicians overseeing the trial had been hardened by my influence. No amount of divinely inspired words could break through the barrier of their allegiance to me. Peter was tried and found guilty, his fate sealed. Yet, even in the face of impending death, he stood firm. His final words melted the hearts of even more souls, turning them to believers in Christ. He was martyred, his body taken by the faithful and laid to rest in a prominent family's burial sarcophagus. In his death, the leaders unwittingly ignited an undercurrent of resentment.

The persecution only fueled the growth of Peter's ministry, sparking a tide that would become the beginning of Roman Christianity. Despite the severe trials and tribulations, the movement expanded throughout the Mediterranean regions. It would be centuries later when the mother of the Eastern Roman Emperor converted to Christianity, She explained the meaning of Constantine's vision. Constantine, would have a vision of victory under the banner of Christ. She embraced Christianity and influenced her son to declare it the sole religion of the empire. The Council of Nicaea was called, and the canon of the Bible was established. Simon Peter, the rock on which the faith was built, had laid the groundwork for what would become the Holy Roman Church. His ministry became the foundation for millions of Christians who followed the teachings of Jesus Christ.

The devil, incensed by the outcome of the trial, fought relentlessly to pervert the spread of this religion. He made it his solemn mission to corrupt as many followers as he could, sowing seeds of doubt and leading them astray from the path of salvation. But the power of faith prevailed. The flame of Christ's message continued to burn bright, illuminating the hearts of believers throughout the ages. Despite the devil's relentless efforts, the message of love and redemption persevered, offering hope and salvation to all who embraced it.

The narrative now unfolds to reveal the compassionate heart of Philip, one of the chosen apostles of Jesus. In the celestial realm, the angel and the Devil engage in a subtle dance of influence, their voices echoing through the depths of Philip's soul.

The angel, with a voice filled with compassion and tenderness, imparts his wisdom to Philip. "Let your heart be a vessel of love and empathy, Philip. Embrace the teachings of Jesus and extend compassion to all those you encounter. Through your acts of kindness, you can heal the broken, uplift the downtrodden, and bring hope to the despairing." But the Devil, with a cunning and manipulative tone, seeks to corrupt Philip's compassion. "Your empathy is a weakness, Philip. It will only lead to disappointment and exploitation. Harden your heart and protect yourself from the pain of others. Focus on your own interests and let the world fend for itself." Yet, the angel's voice persists, cutting through the Devil's deceit. "Let your compassion be a beacon of light, Philip. In your kindness, you will find strength, not weakness. Show mercy to the suffering, forgiveness to the wayward, and love to all. Your acts of compassion will ripple through the world, transforming lives and revealing the depth of God's grace." The Devil, relentless in his pursuit, continues his insidious whispers. "Your efforts are futile, Philip. The world is filled with suffering and pain. What difference can one compassionate soul make? Abandon your foolish endeavors and embrace a world where self interest reigns." But Philip, with a heart brimming with empathy, heeds the angel's call. He walks the path of compassion, extending a helping hand to the marginalized, sharing the message of love and forgiveness. Through his acts of kindness, he touches the lives of the broken, offering them a glimmer of hope in the midst of their struggles. As I chronicle Philip's compassionate journey, the angel and the Devil continue their timeless battle. The angel's voice resonates with grace and tenderness, while the Devil's voice grows increasingly frustrated, his plans of sowing apathy and indifference thwarted at every turn.

Chapter 25
Pillip's
Compassion

In distant lands, Philip's acts of compassion became legendary. He healed the sick, fed the hungry, and offered solace to the weary. Miracles accompanied his steps, a testament to the divine power working through him. Lives were transformed, darkness was dispelled, and the world witnessed the embodiment of Christ's love.

In the shadows, the Devil seethed with envy and resentment. His influence waned as Philip's compassion shone a light on the darkness that plagued humanity. Yet, he remained undeterred, plotting new strategies to corrupt the hearts of the faithful and undermine the power of love. As Philip concluded his compassionate endeavors and rejoined his fellow apostles, the angel whispered, "Your acts of compassion have touched the lives of many, Philip. Your willingness to extend love and mercy has brought healing to the broken and restored hope to the despairing. Your legacy will endure."

The Devil, seething with anger, vowed to intensify his efforts. His hatred burned hotter, fueling his determination to extinguish the flame of compassion that Philip had ignited. The cosmic conflict between light and darkness continued, with each apostle's journey shaping the destiny of humanity.

As I continue my saga of the apostle Philip, I am struck by the profound impact of compassion in a world filled with pain and suffering. Philip's gentle heart serves as a testament to the power of love, while the forces of evil plot their next move. The tale carries onward, with the angel and the Devil preparing for the next stage of their eternal battle, and the apostles poised to face new trials and triumphs in the name of their Lord.

As Mary meticulously transcribed Philip's tale, she couldn't help but feel a deep sense of awe at the divine providence that brought him into the fold of Jesus's disciples. She imagined the transformative moment when Philip first encountered the Son of God, his heart stirred with a profound sense of purpose and destiny. In the days that followed, Philip underwent a profound spiritual transformation. He immersed himself in Jesus's teachings, absorbing the wisdom and love that flowed from his lips. Through intimate conversations and shared experiences, Philip developed a deep bond with the other disciples, forging a sense of camaraderie and unity that would sustain them in their future endeavors.

But Philip's preparation extended beyond the realm of spiritual nourishment. He honed his skills as a communicator, learning to articulate the profound truths of Jesus's message with clarity and conviction. He observed Jesus's interactions with people from all walks of life, witnessing the transformative power of his compassion and love. It was in these moments that Philip realized the magnitude of his calling to share the life-changing message of Jesus with the world.

As Mary delved deeper into Philip's preparation, she discovered the countless hours he spent in prayer and meditation, seeking guidance from the Holy Spirit. Philip understood the importance of aligning his heart and mind with the divine will, for he knew that he would face immense challenges and opposition in his mission to spread the gospel. Mary couldn't help but be captivated by the intimate conversations Philip had with his guardian angel. She marveled at the wisdom and insight that flowed between them, as the angel provided guidance, encouragement, and protection. It was through this divine connection that Philip found solace and strength in times of doubt and uncertainty.

With each passing day, Philip's sense of purpose grew stronger. He knew that he was called to be a light in the darkness, to proclaim the transformative power of Jesus's message to all who would listen. Mary could sense the burning passion within him, the unyielding resolve to fulfill his mission, no matter the cost. The time came for Philip to step out of the familiar comforts of Bethsaida and embark on his journey. He bid farewell to his family and friends, embracing the uncertainty and challenges that lay ahead. Mary could feel the weight of the unknown pressing upon Philip's shoulders, but she also sensed the unwavering faith that fortified his spirit.

As Philip ventured into the unknown, Mary continued to record his encounters and experiences. She chronicled the moments of triumph, as Philip's words resonated with the hearts of those who were seeking truth and meaning. She also documented the trials and tribulations, the skepticism and resistance that he encountered along the way. Through it all, Philip remained steadfast, his unwavering faith shining like a beacon in the darkness.

Mary's heart swelled with pride and admiration as she bore witness to the incredible journey of Philip. She marveled at his dedication, his unwavering commitment to the message of Jesus, and his tireless efforts to spread the light of salvation to all corners of the world. As she concluded this chapter of Philip's story, she couldn't help but feel a renewed sense of purpose in her own role as the recorder of the apostles' tales.

Chapter 26
Chieftan of Scythia

With anticipation and a deep sense of reverence, Mary prepared to embark on the next chapter of this extraordinary journey. She knew that there were many more trials and triumphs to be chronicled, as the apostles ventured forth to fulfill their divine calling. And with each chapter, the legacy of Jesus and his message would be etched deeper into the annals of history, inspiring generations to come. As Philip's journey through Scythia continued, Mary diligently recorded the trials and triumphs of his encounters, capturing the essence of his unwavering faith and the challenges he faced.

From her post in Jerusalem, she felt the weight of responsibility to document these pivotal moments that would shape the course of Christianity. In the shadows, the devil watched with bated breath, seething with fury at the chieftain's conversion. Seeking to spoil Philip's work, the devil whispered doubts and temptations in the chieftain's ear, attempting to lure him away from the path of righteousness. But Philip, guided by the Holy Spirit, stood firm in his convictions, leading the chieftain through the darkness and into the light of Jesus's love. Mary chronicled the intense conversations between Philip and the chieftain, capturing the clash of beliefs and the transformative power of God's grace. She recounted the doubts that plagued the chieftain's mind, the internal struggle he faced in letting go of his former beliefs. But Philip's unwavering dedication and the divine protection that surrounded him gave the chieftain the strength to overcome his fears and embrace the truth.

The devil, enraged by Philip's success, intensified his efforts to undermine the mission. He whispered lies and deceit, attempting to sow seeds of doubt among the Scythian people. But Philip's steadfastness and the unwavering support of his guardian angel shielded him from the devil's schemes. The chieftain, now a fervent believer, became a pillar of strength, defending the message of Jesus and leading his people towards salvation. In her detailed account, Mary vividly portrayed the transformative impact of the chieftain's conversion. She captured the joy and celebration that swept through the Scythian community as they embraced the teachings of Jesus. The devil, witnessing the growing faith and unity among the people, seethed with frustration, knowing that his efforts were being thwarted at every turn .

As the chapter drew to a close, Mary marveled at the profound change that had taken place in the chieftain's heart. She understood the significance of this conversion, not only for the Scythian community but for the spread of Christianity as a whole. The devil's presence lingered in the shadows, his rage fueled by the knowledge that his influence was diminishing in the face of unwavering faith and divine protection.

Chapter 27
The Unknown Territory Scythia

Scythia, an expansive and diverse land, awaited Philip's arrival. From the rugged mountains to the vast steppes, he navigated through unfamiliar terrain, encountering nomadic tribes and diverse cultures along the way. The challenges of language barriers and cultural differences tested his adaptability and his ability to effectively communicate the message of Jesus.

Mary's account of Philip's journey through Scythia was filled with awe-inspiring tales of resilience and determination. She vividly captured the scenes of untamed landscapes, the breathtaking beauty of the mountains, and the vastness of the steppes. Each step brought Philip closer to the hearts of the Scythian people, as he embraced the unknown territory with unwavering faith.

As Philip ventured deeper into Scythia, he faced the daunting task of bridging the gap between cultures. The language barriers presented a formidable challenge, but his genuine compassion and desire to connect with the Scythian people transcended words. Through gestures, expressions, and shared experiences, Philip forged bonds of understanding and trust.

Mary depicted the remarkable encounters Philip had with nomadic tribes, where he was welcomed into their tents and shared meals with them. Through these intimate moments, Philip discovered the universal language of love and kindness that transcended cultural boundaries. He witnessed the Scythian people's curiosity and hunger for spiritual truth, and he seized every opportunity to share the message of Jesus with passion and authenticity.

One particular encounter stood out in Mary's account: the meeting with a wise elder of a Scythian tribe. This elder, adorned with intricate symbols and deep spiritual wisdom, recognized the profound truth in Philip's teachings. Their dialogue, a dance of words and gestures, was a testament to the power of human connection and the universality of the human experience.

Through Mary's retelling, the readers could feel the tension as Philip faced skepticism and resistance from those deeply rooted in their traditional beliefs. The religious authorities, threatened by the influence Philip was gaining among the Scythian people, sought to undermine his message and sow seeds of doubt. But Philip's unwavering faith and the unwavering support of his guardian angel strengthened his resolve to persevere.

Mary captured the suspenseful moments of Philip's encounters with those who opposed his mission. She painted vivid scenes of intense debates and fiery confrontations, where Philip defended the truth of Jesus's message with wisdom and eloquence. The readers could sense the electric atmosphere as the clash of ideologies unfolded, with the fate of countless souls hanging in the balance.

But amidst the challenges and opposition, Mary highlighted the triumphs that Philip experienced. She chronicled the miraculous healings, the transformative moments when lives were forever changed by the power of Jesus's love. These acts of divine intervention served as a powerful testament to the authenticity of Philip's message and the presence of God's grace in the midst of uncertainty.

As the journey through Scythia continued, Philip's dedication and unwavering commitment to his mission shone through. Mary beautifully captured the essence of his character: the humility, the resilience, and the deep love for the Scythian people. She portrayed the moments of joy and celebration as individuals and communities embraced the message of Jesus, finding solace and hope in the midst of their nomadic existence.

With each passing day, Philip's influence grew, and the seeds of faith he planted took root in the hearts of the Scythian people. Mary marveled at the profound impact Philip had, not only on individuals but also on the collective consciousness of an entire region. The Scythian tribes began to embrace the transformative power of Jesus's love, and communities of believers sprouted amidst the vast steppes.

As Mary concluded this chapter of Philip's journey, she couldn't help but be filled with a sense of wonder and anticipation for what lay ahead. The unknown territory of Scythia had become a canvas upon which the message of Jesus was painted, and Philip's unwavering faith had brought light to the darkest corners of the land.

Chapter 28
The Forbidden City's Secret

The tale now shifts its focus to Andrew, one of the lesser-known yet deeply devoted apostles. In the celestial realm, the angel and the Devil engaged in a silent struggle, their voices echoing through the corridors of Andrew's consciousness. The angel, with unwavering conviction, whispered to Andrew, "Embrace your calling, Andrew, for you have been chosen to carry the light of Christ to distant lands. Your courage will be tested, but your unwavering faith will guide you through the darkest of trials. Trust in the divine guidance that will lead you to the souls yearning for salvation."

The Devil, with a sneer of disdain, hissed into Andrew's thoughts, "Why bother with such arduous journeys? Stay within the comforts of your familiar surroundings. Your efforts will be in vain, and your faith will crumble under the weight of adversity." But the angel's voice grew stronger, resonating within Andrew's heart, "Do not falter, Andrew. The love of Christ burns brightly within you. Your humility and unwavering devotion will pierce the darkness, illuminating the path for those lost in despair." The Devil, ever persistent, launched his final attack, "You are insignificant, Andrew. Your efforts will be forgotten, and your message will fall upon deaf ears. Abandon this futile mission and return to the safety of mediocrity." With his heart ablaze with divine purpose, Andrew pushed aside the doubts sown by the Devil. He embarked on a courageous journey, traveling far and wide, carrying the Gospel to the distant lands of China.

As I chronicled Andrew's odyssey, the angel and the Devil engaged in their timeless battle. The angel's voice echoed with encouragement and hope, while the Devil's voice grew increasingly frustrated, his plans of discouragement thwarted at every turn. In distant lands, Andrew's unwavering conviction touched the hearts of those who had long yearned for spiritual truth. Miracles followed in his wake, affirming the divine power of the Gospel he carried. The seeds of faith were sown, and the flame of Christ's love spread throughout Scythia, then into China as his sojourn continued, piercing the darkness that had shrouded the souls of its inhabitants. Through treacherous terrains and encounters with hostile tribes, Andrew pressed on, fortified by the unyielding strength of his faith.

As Andrew stepped through the ancient gates of the Forbidden City, an ethereal hush fell upon the surroundings. The air crackled with an otherworldly energy, as if the spirits of past emperors whispered secrets into the wind. This mystical place, shrouded in opulence and power, held the key to Andrew's next chapter in spreading the message of Jesus.

In the midst of the bustling city, Andrew's eyes fell upon a sick man lying by the side of the road. The man's frail form trembled with weakness, his eyes filled with despair. Without hesitation, Andrew approached him, laying his hands upon the man's forehead and praying for divine healing. A surge of warmth enveloped the sick man's body, coursing through his veins like a healing elixir. The debilitating illness that had plagued him for years vanished, replaced by strength and vitality. The man's eyes widened with astonishment as he realized he stood in the presence of a miracle. Andrew, his voice filled with gratitude, spoke to the healed man, "You have witnessed the power of Jesus, my friend. May His love guide your steps, and may you be a beacon of hope for others." Unbeknownst to Andrew, the man he had healed was none other than the eldest son of the Chinese emperor, the heir to the throne. News of the miraculous healing spread throughout the palace, reaching the ears of the emperor himself. Filled with gratitude and curiosity, the emperor ordered Andrew's accommodation within the palace walls, a rare privilege reserved only for the most esteemed guests.

Within the palace's opulent halls, Andrew found himself in the presence of the emperor and his son, surrounded by courtiers and high-ranking officials. The emperor, moved by the devotion Andrew had shown in saving his firstborn son, granted him an audience, eager to learn more about this foreign faith that had brought about such a wondrous healing. The emperor, his eyes filled with awe, spoke to Andrew, "Your act of compassion has brought light into our lives. Teach me of this Jesus and His teachings, so that I may understand the source of such miracles."

In the quiet moments that followed, the emperor's son, now a fervent believer in Jesus, revealed his conversion to his closest friend within the palace. Together, they sought Andrew's presence in secret, hungry for the transformative power of the gospel. With each clandestine meeting, Andrew's ministry gained strength. The son's friend, touched by Andrew's words, became a staunch advocate of the newfound faith. Under the veil of darkness, they shared the message with trusted confidants, forming the first Christian groups within the walls of the Forbidden City. Andrew, his voice filled with conviction, addressed the small gathering, "Let us find solace in the love of Jesus, even in the midst of secrecy. For in unity, we shall overcome all obstacles."

As Andrew's influence grew, so did the Devil's ire. The palace's religious and political leaders, threatened by the spread of this foreign faith, conspired to undermine Andrew's efforts. Yet, his guardian angel remained steadfast, shielding him from harm and revealing the Devil's machinations. Protected by divine intervention, Andrew was bestowed with the gift of tongues and discernment. He perceived a path to a Christian Chinese method of worship that would integrate harmoniously with the existing beliefs and rituals. This unique fusion, centuries later, would be discovered by Nestorius, who traveled to China with a copy of the Gospel of Thomas, continuing Andrew's legacy and establishing his own brand of Christianity. Andrew, his voice filled with wisdom, imparted his vision to his devoted followers, "Let us embrace the beauty of diversity and adapt our worship to the hearts and minds of the Chinese people. In unity and understanding, we shall forge a new path of faith." Through Nestorius and his followers, Andrew's message of salvation took root and flourished within China. The influence of this evolving faith allowed the message of Jesus to grow and adapt, blending seamlessly with the rich tapestry of Chinese culture, beliefs, and rituals. The gospel spread like wildfire, offering hope, solace, and the promise of everlasting joy and harmony, just as the students of Zen meditated to acquire.

Within the gilded walls of the Forbidden City, a battle of power and influence raged. The dignitaries, once held in high esteem, found their positions threatened by the rising popularity of Andrew's teachings. The Devil, sensing their jealousy and fear, used their vulnerability as a tool to thwart Andrew's mission. In the shadows, the Devil's whispers echoed through the corridors, planting seeds of doubt and division among the palace dignitaries. He spoke in hushed tones, stoking their envy and igniting their desire to eradicate the foreign faith that threatened their authority.

Mary Magdalene, aware of the struggles faced by Andrew within the Forbidden City, gathered her congregation in Jerusalem. She shared the tale of Andrew's heroism and the tribulations he faced in the distant land of China. Her voice resonated with conviction as she described the Devil's machinations and the unwavering faith that propelled Andrew forward. As the news reached the congregation, a sense of sorrow and concern enveloped their hearts. They prayed fervently for Andrew's safety and for the triumph of truth over the forces of darkness.

The Holy Spirit, ever present among them, brought comfort and strength, instilling in them the unwavering resolve to support Andrew from afar. Amidst the growing tension within the Forbidden City, Andrew found himself kidnapped by those who sought to silence his voice. As news of his disappearance spread, the emperor's son, filled with righteous fury, embarked on a relentless search to find his friend and mentor. The emperor's son, his eyes burning with determination, vowed to bring justice to those who had dared to harm Andrew. With a band of loyal followers by his side, he tore through the city, leaving no stone unturned in his quest for answers. Finally, the truth emerged that shattered the son's heart and soul. He discovered Andrew, martyred and tortured for his unwavering faith. The sight of his beloved friend, hanging upside down outside the gates of the palace, ignited a fire within the son's spirit. Grief-stricken yet filled with resolve, the emperor's son orchestrated a magnificent funeral procession, honoring Andrew's sacrifice. In a breach of royal etiquette, he laid Andrew to rest within the tomb of the emperor's family, a final act of defiance against those who had sought to extinguish his light.

Chapter 29
Faith in the Forbidden City

With Andrew's passing, the son's sorrow deepened, but his commitment to the teachings of Jesus remained unwavering. The Holy Spirit, in a profound moment of divine intervention, became his guardian spirit, offering words of wisdom and guidance. The son, his voice resonating with newfound strength, proclaimed to the palace dignitaries, "The path of Jesus holds the key to true enlightenment and salvation. Let us cast aside the chains of our old beliefs and embrace the transformative power of His love."

The son's words resonated with those who had long clung to the teachings of Zen and Confucianism. The Holy Spirit granted him the gift of discernment, allowing him to speak directly to the hearts of the staunchest supporters of the ancient philosophies. His words, infused with divine wisdom, shattered their resistance and opened the door to a new understanding. And so, within the walls of the Forbidden City, the son became a beacon of light, leading a quiet revolution of faith. One by one, the palace dignitaries and influential figures succumbed to the transformative power of the gospel, embracing a Christianity that merged harmoniously with their ancient traditions.

As the message of Jesus echoed through the hallowed halls of the Forbidden City, a profound shift occurred. The palace, once a stronghold of power and opulence, transformed into a sanctuary of love, compassion, and enlightenment. In the midst of turmoil and persecution, the legacy of Andrew's sacrifice lived on. The Holy Spirit continued to guide the son, empowering him to carry the message of Jesus throughout the palace and into the hearts of the Chinese people. And so, dear reader, let us marvel at the triumph of faith over darkness, the resilience of the human spirit, and the power of divine intervention.

As Andrew concluded his journey and was discovered, martyred and tortured before being hung upside down outside the gates of the palace, he had a magnificent funeral procession. They placed him in the tomb of the emperor's family as an unheard-of breach of royal etiquette. In his sorrow, the son of the emperor spoke of how he vowed to continue spreading the message of Jesus throughout the palace and into China. The angel whispered to the son about Andrew's deeds, "Andrew's courage has ignited a flame of faith in the hearts of many. Andrew, your steadfast devotion and unwavering spirit have brought light to a darkened land. You have fulfilled your divine calling with valor and grace." The Devil, defeated in this chapter of the celestial conflict, seethed with rage. His plans had been thwarted, but he knew he would return, his nefarious designs evolving with each setback.

As I concluded the evening's writing on the parchment that was growing larger every day, I sat in my room alone except for the reassuring presence of my guardian angel as it related these tales of Andrew and his victory for the faith of Christianity. He had started in the most mysterious city that the world had no idea existed outside its walls. In Jerusalem, I again felt awe and marveled at the interplay between the angel and the Devil, their ceaseless struggle for dominion over the hearts and minds of humanity.

Andrew's courageous journey was just one chapter in the cosmic drama unfolding, with each apostle leaving an indelible mark on the world. The forces of light and darkness were locked in an eternal battle for the souls of mankind. The tale continued, and with each passing chapter, the stakes grew higher. The angel and the Devil prepared for the next phase of their timeless conflict, where new challenges, triumphs, and revelations awaited the disciples of Christ. The battle between good and evil raged on, shaping the destiny of the apostles and leaving an indelible mark on the course of history.

And so, dear reader, as we witness Andrew's journey within the enigmatic Forbidden City, let us marvel at the intertwining of divine providence and human resilience. May his tale inspire us to embrace the spiritual mysteries that lie within our own lives and to find unity amidst the diversity that enriches our faith.

Chapter 30

Thomas and The Stone Crosses of Mylapore

In the bustling streets of Jerusalem, I found solace in my quiet room, where I would retreat to record the wondrous tale of Thomas's journey to far-off India. As I took up my quill, the voice of my guardian angel whispered in my ear, guiding me on what to write. "Mary," my angel spoke with gentle authority, "recount the remarkable story of Thomas and his impact on the people of Mylapore. Describe the stone crosses he engraved and their significance as symbols of faith and hope." I closed my eyes, envisioning the stone crosses standing proudly in the land of India. They were more than mere engravings; they were sacred emblems of the enduring love of Christ. Each time Thomas etched a cross, he instilled it with the power to uplift the spirits of those who beheld it.

As I chronicled the events, I remembered the words of Thomas as he shared his vision with a group of new believers. "This cross is not just an engraving," he said, "it is a symbol of our faith, our unyielding belief in the teachings of Christ. Each time you see it, remember the sacrifice He made for us." The people of Mylapore marveled at this new form of worship. For them, it was a miraculous manifestation of God's power. Each stone cross bore the weight of this awe and respect, becoming anchors for their fledgling faith. It was a testament to Thomas's unwavering dedication and the transformative power of the message he carried.

In the depths of the night, as I contemplated Thomas's spiritual insights, my guardian angel continued to guide my hand, urging me to describe the significance of the Gospel he composed. "Mary," my angel whispered softly, "reveal the profound teachings within the Gospel of Thomas. Share the mystical interpretations that will ignite the hearts and minds of those who seek truth." The Gospel of Thomas, a treasure trove of divine wisdom, bore witness to Thomas's deep understanding of Christ's teachings. As I delved into his words, I marveled at the profound nature of the revelations he had received. "The Kingdom of God is within you," Thomas wrote, echoing the profound truths revealed to him. His gospel, rediscovered nineteen centuries later along with the Gospel of Mary Magdalene among the Nag Hammadi codices, was filled with enigmatic sayings that invited seekers to contemplate the mysteries of faith. I recorded the teachings of Thomas, the whispers of his words echoing in my mind. Each passage contained a gem of enlightenment, inviting readers to explore the depths of their souls and connect with the divine essence within.

With each new chapter, my connection with Thomas deepened, even as he journeyed through distant lands. Through the whispers of my guardian angel, I was made aware of the miraculous healings that occurred at Thomas's touch. "Mary," my angel spoke with a touch of awe, "convey the power of Thomas's healing ministry. Describe the profound impact it had on the lives of the sick and suffering." Thomas possessed a divine gift, the ability to channel the healing energy of Christ. As he laid his hands upon the afflicted, ailments were vanquished, and hope was restored. The blind saw, the deaf heard, and the crippled walked. I recorded the accounts of healing, the restoration of health, and the hope that blossomed in the hearts of the afflicted. Each miraculous encounter was a testament to the boundless compassion and power of Christ, working through the hands of His devoted apostle.

"Mary," my angel whispered, "unveil the sacred exchanges between Thomas and the seekers of wisdom. Share the profound truths that were revealed in these encounters." In the ancient temples of India, Thomas engaged in dialogues with learned scholars and seekers of truth. He expounded on the teachings of Christ, weaving them with the rich tapestry of Eastern philosophy. The result was a harmonious fusion of faith and knowledge, resonating deeply with those who longed for spiritual enlightenment. I recorded the profound conversations, the exchange of ideas that sparked new insights and expanded the horizons of knowledge. Thomas's words resonated with the seekers, bridging the gap between cultures and beliefs, and opening new pathways to understanding.

As Thomas continued his ministry in India, the forces of opposition grew stronger. The devil, threatened by the light that Thomas brought to the land, conspired to extinguish it. But my guardian angel shielded me from the malevolent presence, allowing me to record the trials and triumphs of Thomas's journey. "Mary," my angel spoke with determination, "depict the fierce resistance Thomas faced. Unveil the sacrifices he made and the ultimate price he paid for his unwavering faith." Thomas faced persecution, threats, and eventually, martyrdom. The forces of darkness sought to silence his voice and eradicate his teachings. Yet, he stood firm, his unwavering faith undiminished. I chronicled the final moments of Thomas's earthly journey, his unwavering resolve in the face of adversity, and the eternal legacy he left behind. The flame of martyrdom illuminated the path for future generations, inspiring them to stand strong in their faith, regardless of the trials they faced. As each chapter concluded, the Devil's fury intensified, for he recognized the power of these tales to ignite the souls of believers and strengthen their faith. Yet, my guardian angel remained vigilant, shielding me from the malevolent forces, and ensuring the sanctity of the stories that unfolded within my words. The saga of Thomas's journey continued to unfold, his encounters and teachings leaving an indelible mark on the landscape of faith. And I, as the chronicler, bore witness to the cosmic battle between light and darkness, recording the triumphs and trials of those who dared to carry the message of Christ to the corners of the world.

Chapter 31
The Boldness of James the Less

The unfolding saga now turned its attention to James the Less, one of the lesser-known apostles. Within the celestial realm, the angel and the Devil engaged in a battle of influence, their voices echoing through the corridors of James' thoughts and aspirations. The angel, his voice resolute yet gentle, whispered to James, "Embrace the courage within you, for you are chosen to bear witness to the transformative power of Christ's teachings. Let go of your insecurities and step into the light of your divine purpose. Through your words and actions, you can ignite a flame of faith in the hearts of many."

But the Devil, the master of doubt and deception, sought to sow seeds of fear and uncertainty within James' soul. He whispered, "You are insignificant, overshadowed by the other apostles. Why bother with this risky path? Remain in the shadows, where it is safe and comfortable."

The angel's voice persisted, undeterred by the Devil's attempts to dissuade James. "Do not underestimate the impact you can make,

James," the angel encouraged. "Your humility and unwavering devotion to the message of Christ can touch the lives of those who feel overlooked and forgotten. Through your gentle strength, you can bring hope to the weary souls."

But the Devil, crafty and manipulative, continued his assault on James' resolve. He whispered, "You are not worthy of this calling. Doubt will be your constant companion, and failure will be your fate. Give in to your fears, and let them consume you."

In the depths of his inner struggle, James turned his gaze inward, seeking the truth amidst the conflicting voices. He felt the tug of the Holy Spirit within him, urging him to rise above his insecurities and embrace the boldness that lay dormant within his being. With renewed determination, James chose to heed the angel's call. He stepped out of the shadows, his heart filled with the fire of conviction. Through his words and actions, he would bear witness to the love and grace of Jesus Christ, defying the Devil's attempts to undermine his purpose.

As I chronicled James' journey, the angel and the Devil continued their ongoing debate. The angel's voice echoed with encouragement and faith, while the Devil's voice grew increasingly frustrated, his plans for sowing doubt and discord thwarted once again. The cosmic battle between light and darkness played out within the hearts and minds of the apostles, each step they took a testament to their courage and unwavering faith. The angel and the Devil, locked in a perpetual struggle, fought for the souls of humanity, their influence shaping the destiny of the disciples.

As I concluded the chapter, I marveled at the intricate dance between the angel and the Devil, their relentless pursuit of victory over one another. The narrative of redemption unfolded through the lives of the apostles, their individual stories intertwined with the celestial conflict that raged on. The journey of the apostles continued, and with each passing moment, the stakes grew higher. The angel and the Devil prepared for the next episode in the epic saga, where new trials and triumphs awaited the disciples of Christ. The battle between good and evil raged on, leaving an indelible mark on the hearts and minds of those touched by the apostles' mission.

The Humility of Thaddeus:

The celestial tapestry now shifted its focus to Thaddeus, one of the lesser-known apostles whose humility and gentle spirit carried a profound impact on those he encountered. The angel and the Devil engaged in a thought-provoking conversation, their voices entwined with the unfolding narrative, exploring the depth of Thaddeus' humility and its transformative power. The angel, his voice soft and comforting, whispered to Thaddeus, "Embrace your innate humility, Thaddeus, for it is a precious gift. Through your unassuming nature, you reflect the very essence of Christ's teachings. Let your humility be a beacon of light, drawing others closer to the love and grace of Jesus."

But the Devil, the master of pride and arrogance, sought to undermine Thaddeus' humility, whispering words of self-doubt and insignificance. "Why bother with your humble ways, Thaddeus?" the Devil sneered. "You will be overlooked and forgotten amidst the grandeur of the other apostles. Rise up, assert yourself, and make a name for yourself."

The angel's voice persisted, unwavering in its message of humility's power. "Do not underestimate the impact of your gentle spirit, Thaddeus," the angel assured. "Your humility opens hearts, dismantles barriers, and fosters unity. Through your unassuming ways, you embody the very essence of Jesus' servant leadership."

Thaddeus listened intently, caught in the struggle between humility and pride. The conflicting voices resonated within him, challenging his understanding of his role as an apostle. In moments of introspection and prayer, he sought divine guidance, yearning to align his heart with the essence of Christ's humility.

As I chronicled Thaddeus' journey, the celestial debate between the angel and the Devil continued to unfold. Their arguments echoed in Thaddeus' thoughts, inviting him to examine the true nature of humility and its transformative potential in a world marred by ego and self-centeredness. Meanwhile, in the quiet solitude of her chamber, Mary Magdalene engaged in a heartfelt conversation with her guardian angel. They delved into the depths of Thaddeus' humility, seeking to understand its profound impact on those who encountered his gentle presence. "Angel of wisdom, illuminate the essence of Thaddeus' humility," Mary implored her celestial companion. "Help me grasp the significance of his unassuming nature and how it can inspire others to embody the virtues of Christ. Show me how his humility can lead to the healing of broken spirits and foster unity among the disciples."

The angel, with profound insight, responded, "Mary, witness the humility of Thaddeus. In his unassuming ways, he brings comfort to the brokenhearted, extends compassion to the marginalized, and bridges divides among the disciples. His humility is a testament to the servant heart of Jesus, leading others to embrace the path of selflessness and unity."

With each passing day, Thaddeus walked in humble service, embodying the virtues of Christ. His gentle presence and willingness to serve others with humility touched lives and transformed hearts. Through his actions, he became a living testament to the power of humility in a world longing for authentic love and compassion.

As the episode neared its conclusion, Mary reflected on her conversation with her guardian angel. The insights gained offered a profound understanding of the transformative nature of humility. The interplay between the angel and the Devil continued to shape Thaddeus' journey, as the celestial conflict raged on.

The Zeal of Simon the Zealot:

Amidst a world filled with political unrest and simmering rebellion, Simon the Zealot emerged as an apostle consumed by fervent zeal. His journey intertwined with the unfolding narrative of resistance and defiance against oppressive forces. The celestial realm watched as the angel and the Devil engaged in a charged dialogue, reflecting the inner turmoil of Simon. The angel, with a voice resonating with unwavering conviction, implored Simon, "Channel your zeal into righteous action, Simon. Let your passion for justice fuel your commitment to the teachings of Christ. Rise against injustice, but temper your fervor with wisdom and compassion. Unite the oppressed and the downtrodden, and forge a path of liberation."

But the Devil, with his cunning words, sought to manipulate Simon's zeal for his own wicked purposes. "Embrace your anger and unleash it upon your enemies, Simon. Seek vengeance and retribution. Let your zeal consume you and drive you to violence. Use your passion to sow chaos and discord."

The angel's voice persisted, an unwavering beacon of divine guidance. "Do not let your zeal blind you, Simon. Seek justice, but remember the importance of mercy and forgiveness. Let your passion inspire change through peaceful means. Use your voice to unite, not to divide. In this way, your zeal will become a force for good."

But the Devil, the master of deception, continued to exploit Simon's righteous anger. "Why settle for peaceful resistance when violence can achieve immediate results? Embrace the power of your zeal to strike fear into the hearts of your enemies. Let the world tremble before your wrath."

In the depths of his inner struggle, Simon wrestled with the conflicting voices. He pondered the path of righteous rebellion and the temptation of vengeance. He sought to find the delicate balance between fervor and compassion, understanding that true liberation is born from unity and love.

As the chapter drew to a close, the angel and the Devil continued their battle of influence, their voices echoing through the annals of history.

The Courage of Bartholomew:

In the shadowy depths of human despair, a flicker of courage emerged, embodied by Bartholomew, one of the lesser-known apostles. The celestial realm trembled with anticipation as the angel and the Devil engaged in a timeless discourse, their words echoing through the corridors of Bartholomew's soul. The angel, his voice resonant and unwavering, imparted words of fortitude to Bartholomew. "Rise above the doubts that seek to ensnare you, for you possess a strength that can inspire others. Embrace the unknown and step into the realm of the miraculous. Your faith will be a beacon of light in the darkest corners of humanity."

But the Devil, his voice insidious and seductive, sought to undermine Bartholomew's resolve. "You are insignificant, a mere shadow among the more prominent apostles. Why venture into the perilous unknown? Stay in the comfort of the familiar, where your fears can be quelled."

The angel persisted, his voice infused with divine wisdom. "Do not underestimate the power of your presence, Bartholomew. Your quiet strength and unwavering loyalty will touch the hearts of those who yearn for hope. Through your humility, you will bring solace to the broken and weary."

But the Devil, cunning and relentless, continued his assault on Bartholomew's faith. "You are not equipped for this journey. Doubt will be your constant companion, and failure will be your fate. Surrender to your fears, and let them consume you."

In the depths of his inner turmoil, Bartholomew turned his gaze inward, searching for the truth amidst the conflicting voices. He felt the stirrings of the Holy Spirit within him, urging him to rise above his insecurities and embrace the courage that lay dormant within his soul. With renewed determination, Bartholomew chose to heed the angel's call. He stepped out of the shadows, his heart filled with the fire of conviction. Through his actions and unwavering faith, he would bear witness to the transformative power of Jesus Christ, defying the Devil's attempts to undermine his purpose.

As I chronicled Bartholomew's journey, the angel and the Devil engaged in an eternal debate. The angel's voice resonated with hope and truth, while the Devil's voice grew increasingly frustrated, his plans to sow doubt and despair thwarted once again. The cosmic battle between light and darkness played out within the hearts and minds of the apostles, each step they took a testament to their courage and unwavering faith. The angel and the Devil, locked in a perpetual struggle, fought for the souls of humanity, their influence shaping the destiny of the disciples.

As I concluded this episode, I marveled at the intricate dance between the angel and the Devil, their relentless pursuit of victory over one another. The narrative of redemption unfolded through the lives of the apostles, their individual stories intertwined with the celestial conflict that raged on.

In foreign lands, James' passionate preaching ignited a fire in the hearts of those who heard his words. Miracles followed in his wake, validating the divine power that accompanied the proclamation of the Gospel. Lives were transformed, darkness was dispelled, and the Kingdom of God expanded its reach. In the shadows, the Devil seethed with rage, his plans of derailing the apostles' mission once again thwarted. Yet, his malevolent presence remained, plotting new strategies to undermine the disciples and plunge the world into despair. As James concluded his fervent endeavors and reunited with his fellow apostles, the angel whispered, "Your zeal has kindled the flames of faith in the hearts of many, James. Your unwavering passion and commitment have brought light to the darkest corners of the world. Your legacy will endure."

The Devil, defeated but far from vanquished, simmers with resentment. His hatred burns brighter, fueling his determination to unleash chaos and discord upon the faithful. The cosmic conflict between light and darkness continues, with each apostle's journey shaping the destiny of humanity. As I conclude this chapter, I am struck by the delicate balance between the angel's guidance and the Devil's malevolence. James' fiery zeal serves as a beacon of hope, while the forces of evil seek to extinguish the light. The tale carries onward, with the angel and the Devil preparing for the next stage of their eternal battle, and the apostles poised to face new trials and triumphs in the name of their Lord.

With each passing day, the churches founded by the apostles expanded, breaking barriers and borders, connecting people across regions. The apostles nurtured these communities with words of encouragement, hope, and love, providing them with a sense of purpose and belonging. In Antioch, where the followers of Jesus were first called Christians, the church became a vibrant community of believers. People from different cultures, races, and classes found solace and unity under the teachings of Jesus Christ. Here, the apostles Peter and

Paul played significant roles in guiding the church and establishing it as a beacon of hope for the followers of Jesus.

The church in Jerusalem, under the leadership of James, the brother of Jesus, also flourished. Despite the frequent threats and persecutions from local authorities, the community remained firm in their faith. The courage and resilience of the believers in the face of adversity were a testament to their unshakable faith and trust in God. Meanwhile, in Rome, the Christian community grew in secret, cautious of the ever-watchful eyes of the Roman authorities. Despite the dangers, the underground church, under the guidance of Peter, saw a steady increase in the number of followers. The willingness of the believers to risk their lives for their faith showed the profound impact of the apostles' teachings. Throughout their journeys, the apostles kept their focus on their divine mission to spread the Gospel and establish the Church. They taught their followers to love one another, serve the needy, and maintain unity in the face of adversity. The Holy Spirit guided them, helping them to face challenges and emerge stronger.

Best
Sellers

The Chronicles of Mary
Magdelene Series

Mary's Salvation
The Illuminated Path
Jerusalem's Faith
Paul's Odyssey
Andrew's Adventures
Mary's Celestial Journey

In the Company

of Angels
John's Journey
Heaven's Warriors
Isabella's Divine Destiny

WRITTEN BY

Steve Taylor
Https://maryschronicles.online

Also By Steve Taylor

Books for people of Faith!
Non-Fiction
The Discovering The Disciples Series
Lost and Found Christianity:Christianity's Lost Sagas
Discovering the Disciple-Volumes 1 and 2
Gnostic versus Christians: the Battle for the new Testament
Apostle's Oddessy: The Untold Tales of ST. Thomas
Phillip in Scythia:Apostle to the Nomads

link:https://discoveringth
edisciples.com

Fiction
The Chronicles of Mary
Magdelene:
Heavens Gate
The Illuminated Path
link:https://heavensgate.o
nline

Study Journals
Your Salvation Journal
Series
Learn,Memorize and
Study one scripture per
journal!
link:https://discover-
ingthedisciples.com
Link:https://heavensgate.
online

Epilogue-the Illuminated Path-Coming Soon

J ust beyond the last flicker of earthly consciousness, the Gate of Heaven stood majestic and resolute. This was not simply an ethereal passageway, but a shimmering, celestial tear in reality that marked the threshold between divinity and humanity. Where others had foretold a divine event, they had not envisioned the breathtaking splendor that unfolded when the Heavens deigned to reveal themselves. This spectacle was the divine spark of God's will reaching into our realm, an event that reshaped our understanding of the cosmos.

Above, where the stars once shone, the celestial rift unfurled a sight more dazzling than the prophets of the old testament could have imagined. It was a dawning of divine brilliance, an event bridging two distinct universes: one resplendent in divine majesty, the other striving to grasp the light of its creator amid the shadows. From my vantage, the heavenly realm was alive with divine energy. Gilded streets stretched out into the distance, fading into an ethereal haze of celestial majesty. The air itself seemed to hum with anticipation, a symphony of harmonics that defied human comprehension. All around, God's dominion shimmered with power, a living, crackling force that was as awe-inspiring as it was humbling.

And then, in a moment of divine synchronicity, the divine plan burst forth. With an explosive eruption of divine energy, a sacred transition began. Like a celestial tide, the brilliant energy of God's grace began to flow through the celestial gate, coalescing around His divine presence. This was the Holy Spirit, the divine spark of God Himself, now preparing to embark on an unprecedented journey into the realm of humanity. Accompanying this divine envoy was a celestial host of angels, radiant beings of pure light, each imbued with a fraction of God's infinite majesty. They watched in reverence as the Holy Spirit prepared to cross into the earthly realm, their faces etched with a determination that spoke of their divine mission.

As the celestial procession started, a profound sense of purpose washed over me. A surge of divine energy coursed through every fiber of my being, an affirmation of the sacred mission we were embarking upon. This was our calling: to escort the Holy Spirit into the realm of mankind, to aid in the divine mission of bringing God's most beloved creation, mankind, back into His grace. There was a sacred exchange in that moment, a divine reciprocation that would change the course of history. The spark of God's divine presence was now manifesting in the physical realm. God's earthly son, Jesus, filled with His divine essence, had offered humanity a path to salvation and grace. This celestial event was God's promise to mankind, a promise of grace, should they accept and believe. The divine spark of Jesus' sacrifice was not merely a gift; it was a divine bridge leading humanity back to the celestial light. And this bridge was not just a path, but a symbol of love, hope, and the triumphant return of lost souls to the heavenly fold.

It was the beginning of a journey, a celestial odyssey that would not only challenge our understanding of divinity but also redefine the connection between God and mankind. As we watched the Holy Spirit's journey unfold, we knew our lives were about to change. In this mission, we were not just observers but active participants in a celestial dance that would shape the very fabric of existence. This was our invitation to you, the reader, to join us in this divine journey: to witness the majesty of the celestial gate, the radiance of the angels, and the inspiring odyssey of the Holy Spirit, as we carry out our divine mission, against all odds, in the name of grace, salvation, and divine love. The journey is just beginning, and we invite you to experience every breathtaking step along the way.

In the moment of divine anticipation, I, the Holy Spirit, hovered at the brink of the celestial rift, curious yet sure of the mission that awaited me. As the divine spark of God, I wielded immense power within the celestial realm. Beyond this tear in the divine fabric, I would command dominion over the beasts and elements. Yet, my ability to aid mankind hinged on their acceptance of the ultimate sacrifice Jesus had made. Without their willing embrace, the sequence of mystical transference could not fully manifest. Silently, I awaited the arrival of Jesus. I knew I would find receptive vessels on the other side of the portal: those who surrounded Jesus, their hearts aflame with faith and resolve. But among them, one stood out: the confidante, one blessed with unparalleled strength and resilience. I knew she held the potential to ensure the flourishing of this nascent religion, to fulfill a divine mission much like Mary, Jesus's mother. This other Mary was chosen for a unique destiny: to faithfully record the odysseys of the apostles, to nurture the beginnings of Christ's ministry. She would counsel, heal, and love the apostles, those precious vessels of sacred words. Even as I waited, I felt a divine certainty that she would become an invaluable cornerstone in this holy endeavor. Yet, while I held this knowledge, my intervention hinged on the spirits of others. It was I who would bring God's peace and love, who would shield them against the fallen one. It was I who would advise the angels on the true meanings of God's orders, and guide their guardianship against the forces of evil. It was I who would manage this cosmic conflict, becoming the administrator of divine battles and defender of righteousness.

The light at the rift grew brighter, the glory of heaven seeping into the realm of man. My journey was just about to begin. I saw Jesus, His head and upper torso emerging from the dazzling light. It was time. In a blinding flash, I passed through the veil and immersed myself into the earthly realm: a world of air and life, so different from the celestial domain. I perceived the apostles for the first time, their hope, fear, and dedication washing over me. And then, there she was: Mary. She would be my sanctuary. As I dispersed to answer the calls of new believers seeking salvation, I would always return to her. In her faith and resolve, I would find refuge. This, I knew, was just the beginning. Through her, I would touch countless lives, bring solace to those in need, and forever change the course of human history.

In the sacred moment when Heaven's Gate was torn asunder, I, the Holy Spirit, moved through the breach from the divine realm into the earthly. The celestial divide, a barrier once impervious, now shattered like fine crystal under the echoing words of the divine prophecy. They had foreseen the rending, the monumental event that would mark my entry into the physical world as Jesus's eternal spark. But the spectacle outshone all prophecy. The glory of the merging universes, divine and human, was a sight to behold, even for an eternal entity like me. It was a world tainted by the actions of a fallen angel, a shadow of God, who deceived Eve and led mankind into a state of sin. Now, I, the Spirit of the same God, traversed the same universe, carrying the essence of

Jesus, returning to its divine source but with a newfound purpose: to serve as a celestial bridge.

As I swept through the rift, I saw them: my first earthly recipients, the apostles. Humble, faithful, and full of divine potential, they were chosen by Jesus himself to carry forth His teachings and His message of salvation. Among them stood Mary, the chosen one. She who bore the blood of Christ and would be the rock upon which His disciples could anchor their faith. Mary, destined to unlock the words of His ministry and document the apostles' odysseys for the future faithful. I saw their paths stretching forth, their trials and tribulations as they carried the light of Christ's teachings to the four corners of the world. Each challenge they faced, every hurdle they overcame, would mold them and, through them, shape the early Church. I saw their courage, their dedication, and their unwavering faith, even in the face of grave adversity. In them, I saw the future of Christianity, bright and resilient, spreading across the globe.

And so, my divine journey in the earthly realm began. Guided by the will of the Creator, I moved among His chosen, ever present and ready to guide, comfort, and empower them in their monumental task. Through them, the message of salvation would spread, and the world would come to know the love of God. Through them, the legacy of Christ would live on, and the early Christian Church would rise. This was their story. This was our story: a divine narrative of faith, sacrifice, and redemption.

In the aftermath of Jesus' ascension and the Holy Spirit's divine outpouring on the Apostles, the humble and resilient Mary found herself in a world reborn. A world set aflame by the divine spark, with hearts longing for salvation, and ears eager for the Gospel's teachings. From Jerusalem to the farthest corners of Gaul, Hispania, Scotland, Britannia, and Germania, Mary embarked on a mission of unprecedented scope and consequence. Her calling? To share the Light of the World and to construct a Church that would outlast the ages. With an unwavering faith and a heart full of God's love, Mary, once a mere spectator of miracles, became an architect of faith. In each land, she erected more than just buildings: she built communities of believers, united by their love for Christ. Even in the face of relentless opposition, the Church stood firm, as if cemented by divine mortar. Mary's successful mission reverberated through history and ultimately shaped the Holy Roman Church.

But this story isn't merely about the rise of the Church. It's about a battle fought not just on earthly grounds, but in the celestial realm, where angels stood guard, shielding the Apostles and their followers from the devil's machinations. It's about the miracles that reached into the heart of every man and woman, from stoic centurions and rugged stonemasons to the richest nobles and humblest peasants. What was Mary's secret weapon? It wasn't just the teachings she carried or the miracles she performed. No, it was the administrative systems she put in place, a network of overseers ensuring the continued flourishing of each fledgling Christian community, that solidified her legacy. These structures allowed the Gospel to reach far and wide, strengthening the bonds between disparate communities and feeding the flames of faith across continents.

Years later, Mary returned to Jerusalem, her mission accomplished. What she had begun was absorbed into the burgeoning Roman Holy Order, eventually becoming the cornerstone of the Holy Roman Church. Today, we look back at Mary's journey with awe, as we realize her role in shaping the world we know now. Mary's story is a testament to the power of faith, the strength of hope, and the triumph of love over adversity. Her life, her struggles, and her victories are a stirring reminder that we, too, are part of an ongoing journey, an epic saga that began with Jesus' ascension and continues till today.

Are you ready to walk with us on this illuminated path? Are you prepared to experience the wonders and miracles that transformed warlords into believers, and the rich and poor alike into disciples of faith? Then delve deeper into the story of Mary, and witness a journey that transcends time, a tale of divine love and celestial warfare, and a mission that changed the world. The battle of the heavens might have ended, but the journey of The Illuminated Path continues, even today. This is your invitation to join that journey.

About the Author

The Author writes and designs Books, Journal and other study guides for Christian Faith Gospel. Inspired by the spirit of Helping others gain insight into the worship and prayer of the gospel of Jesus Christ and his Followers, He has written several books and created many other study materials for Christian bible study.

Breaking *THE* Chains

A guide for abolishing modern day
slavery

STEVE TAYLOR

Bonus Read--Breaking the Chains: A guide for abolishing modern day slavery By Steve Taylor

So enormous, so dreadful, so irredeemable did(slavery's) wickedness
appear that.. I from this time determined that I would never rest
till I affected its abolition",William Wilberforce 1789,

is a call to action we should all
be willing to answer as Christians!

"Breaking the Chain: A Guide to Modern Slavery" is a study guide that explores the biblical teachings on human dignity and the abolition of modern slavery. This guide is designed to help readers gain a deeper understanding of the Christian perspective on this issue and to provide practical tools for action. Whether you are a Christian leader, an activist, or simply someone who cares about justice, this guide will equip you to make a difference in the fight against modern slavery.

As Christians, we are called to be agents of change in the world, to bring light to the darkness and hope to the hopeless. We are to be a force for good in the world, to seek justice, and defend the oppressed. And one of the most pressing challenges of our time is the issue of modern-day slavery. Yes, slavery still exists in our world today, and it's time for us to take action and unchain those who are still in bondage.

But where do we begin? How can we as Christians lead the charge against slavery?

First, we must recognize the reality of the situation. Despite being illegal in every country, slavery still exists in various forms around the world, from forced labor to sex trafficking. It's a global issue that demands a global response.

Second, we need to educate ourselves and others about the issue. We need to understand the root causes of slavery, such as poverty, lack of education, and corruption, and work to address those underlying issues. We also need to recognize the signs of slavery and trafficking and know how to report them to the authorities.

Third, we need to support organizations that are working to combat slavery and provide assistance to survivors. This includes organizations that provide shelter, counseling, job training, and legal services to those who have been freed from slavery.

But perhaps most importantly, we need to approach this issue with a mindset of love and compassion. We need to see those who are enslaved not as statistics or problems to be solved, but as fellow human beings created in the image of God. We need to walk alongside them, listen to their stories, and provide support and encouragement as they begin their journey towards freedom and healing.

In short, we as Christians have a unique opportunity and responsibility to lead the charge against slavery. Let's commit ourselves to this cause, to unchain those who are still in bondage, and to bring hope and freedom to the world.

"Unchained: How Christians Can Lead the Charge Against Slavery"

As Christians, this is especially true when it comes to the issue of slavery, which has been a scourge on humanity for centuries. Today, despite the progress that has been made in abolishing legal slavery, millions of people are still trapped in various forms of modern-day slavery. In modern times, forced labor, human trafficking, and debt bondage are forms of modern-day slavery that continue to plague societies around the world.

These practices are often hidden in plain sight, and their victims are vulnerable people who are lured or forced into exploitation for the profit of others. In this report, we will examine what these practices are, how they are perpetrated, and how the efforts of abolitionists in the past are being undermined by current immigration policies. We will also discuss how Christian values need to be maintained in order to continue the fight against modern-day slavery.

In the face of these challenges, it is essential to maintain Christian values in the fight against slavery. Christian teachings emphasize the importance of treating all people with love, compassion, and respect, regardless of their race, nationality, or social status. Christians believe that all people are created in the image of God and are therefore inherently valuable and deserving of dignity and respect.

In the book of Galatians, chapter 3, verse 28, the apostle Paul writes, "There is neither Jew nor Gentile, neither slave nor free, nor is there male and female, for you are all one in Christ Jesus." This powerful statement has become a cornerstone of Christian theology and speaks to the heart of the message of the Gospel: that all people are equal in the eyes of God, and that we are all called to love and serve one another.

To fully appreciate the significance of Galatians 3:28, it is important to understand the historical and cultural context in which it was written. During the time of Paul, the world was deeply divided along lines of ethnicity, class, and gender. Jews and Gentiles were often at odds with one another, and slavery was an accepted and widely practiced institution in many societies. Women, too, were often treated as second-class citizens, with limited rights and opportunities.

Moreover, the Bible is full of examples of God's concern for the oppressed and marginalized. Jesus himself demonstrated a particular concern for those who were most vulnerable, such as the poor, the sick, and the outcasts of society. As such, Christians have a unique role to play in the fight against modern-day slavery, using their faith as a motivation to work for justice and equality for all.

Today, the message of Galatians 3:28 remains just as relevant and powerful as it was in the time of Paul. We live in a world that is still deeply divided along lines of ethnicity, culture, class, and gender. We see this in the ongoing struggles for racial justice, the persistence of gender inequality,

Here's the transcription with the corrections:

"The Fight for Freedom: Abolitionists in Action"

In the early 19th century, the world was grappling with the evils of slavery. Though slavery had been a common practice for centuries, people were beginning to recognize its horrors. The slave trade had become a lucrative business for many European countries and their colonies. In the midst of this, there were voices that spoke out against slavery and demanded its abolition. One such voice was that of William Wilberforce, a British politician and devout Christian who fought tirelessly for the abolition of slavery.

Wilberforce was deeply influenced by his faith, and his passion for abolition was rooted in his belief in the inherent worth and dignity of all human beings. He believed that slavery was a violation of God's will and that it was the responsibility of Christians to fight against it. He was also inspired by the teachings of 1 John 4:20 and Galatians 3:28, which emphasized the importance of loving all people as brothers and sisters in Christ and rejecting the notion of slavery.

In 1787, Wilberforce founded the Society for Effecting the Abolition of the Slave Trade, which aimed to raise awareness of the atrocities of the slave trade and to lobby for its abolition. He also worked closely with other abolitionists, such as Thomas Clarkson, Granville Sharp, and Hannah More, to gather evidence and make a case against slavery.

Wilberforce's efforts were met with fierce opposition from those who had vested interests in the slave trade. But he persevered, delivering numerous speeches in parliament and presenting bills for the abolition of the slave trade. It took many years, but in 1807, the Slave Trade Act was finally passed, making the British slave trade illegal.

The abolition of the British slave trade had a ripple effect throughout the world, inspiring others to follow suit. In the United States, Christian leaders such as Harriet Beecher Stowe, Frederick Douglass, and William Lloyd Garrison also fought tirelessly for the abolition of slavery. They too were inspired by the teachings of 1 John 4:20 and Galatians 3:28, which had been instrumental in the British abolition movement.

Stowe, in particular, was deeply influenced by the story of Uncle Tom, a slave whose story she chronicled in her famous novel, "Uncle Tom's Cabin." The novel had a profound impact on American society, raising awareness of the brutality of slavery and inspiring many to take action. Stowe's work was also deeply rooted in her faith, and she believed that it was the responsibility of Christians to fight against slavery.

Frederick Douglass was another prominent abolitionist who used his faith as a force for change. As a former slave himself, he had firsthand experience of the horrors of slavery and was determined to fight against it. He believed that slavery was a sin and that it was the responsibility of Christians to put an end to it. Douglass used his powerful oratory skills to speak out against slavery and to call on his fellow Christians to take action.

William Lloyd Garrison was also deeply committed to the abolition of slavery. He believed that it was the responsibility of Christians to fight against slavery and to work towards the establishment of a just and equitable society. Garrison founded the American Anti-Slavery Society, which aimed to raise awareness of the atrocities of slavery and to lobby for its abolition.

Together, these Christian leaders and many others worked tirelessly to bring about the abolition of slavery. They were inspired by the teachings of 1 John 4:20 and Galatians 3:28, which emphasized the importance of loving all people as brothers and sisters in Christ and rejecting the notion of slavery. Their work was instrumental in bringing about the end of slavery in the Western world.

Today, the legacy of these Christian abolitionists lives on. Their commitment to justice and their dedication to the fight...

To summarize, the powerful message of 1 John 4:20 and Galatians 3:28 has had a significant impact on history, particularly in the fight against slavery. The biblical principle of loving all people as brothers and sisters in Christ, regardless of race or social status, inspired Christians such as William Wilberforce and American abolitionists to work tirelessly towards the end of slavery. Through their persistence and dedication, they were able to bring about significant change in their societies and pave the way for a more just and equitable future.

"The Abolitionist's Handbook: Strategies and Solutions for Ending Slavery"

In the 18th and 19th centuries, abolitionists in England and America worked tirelessly to end the transatlantic slave trade and to abolish slavery itself. These individuals were inspired by their Christian values, which taught them that all people were created equal in the eyes of God. They believed it was their duty to fight for the freedom and dignity of every human being.

William Wilberforce, a British politician and devout Christian, was one of the leading abolitionists of his time. His reflections on God's word profoundly changed his character and outlook. In 1789, Wilberforce delivered his first anti-slavery speech before Parliament. He passionately declared, "So enormous, so dreadful, so irredeemable did slavery's wickedness appear that... I determined that I would never rest till I effected its abolition." This sentiment is a call to action that all Christians should heed.

After more than 20 years in Parliament advocating for change, the Slave Trade Act was passed in 1807, making the British slave trade illegal. The ripple effects of this act inspired other nations to follow suit.

In the United States, figures like Frederick Douglass, Harriet Tubman, and William Lloyd Garrison led the abolitionist movement. They too were inspired by Christian teachings. Harriet Beecher Stowe, influenced by the story of Uncle Tom, chronicled his life in her novel,

"Uncle Tom's Cabin." This book raised awareness of slavery's brutality and inspired many Americans to act.

Frederick Douglass, a former slave, used his firsthand experiences to condemn slavery. He believed it was a Christian duty to end such a heinous institution. Likewise, William Lloyd Garrison, founder of the American Anti-Slavery Society, spread the abolitionist message throughout the U.S.

Together, these Christian leaders made significant strides in abolishing slavery in the Western world. Their commitment was grounded in scriptures like 1 John 4:20 and Galatians 3:28, which emphasize loving all people as siblings in Christ.

However, the fight against slavery continues today. Modern forms of slavery, such as forced labor, human trafficking, and debt bondage, persist globally. Current immigration policies in many countries, unfortunately, exacerbate these issues. For instance, U.S. immigration policies often make legal entry difficult, pushing many to take dangerous, illegal routes. This vulnerability can lead to human trafficking and forced labor situations. The U.K. has also seen a rise in challenges for victims of human trafficking due to recent immigration law changes.

In summary, while the 19th-century abolitionists made significant progress in ending slavery, modern forms still exist. Current immigration policies in various countries, such as the U.S. and the U.K., can inadvertently support these exploitative practices. It's essential to recognize and combat these issues, remembering the unwavering commitment of historical figures like Wilberforce and Douglass.

"The Abolitionist's Handbook: Strategies and Solutions for Ending Slavery"

In the 18th and 19th centuries, abolitionists in England and America worked tirelessly to bring an end to the transatlantic slave trade and to abolish slavery itself. These individuals were inspired by their

Christian values, which taught them that all people were created equal in the eyes of God and that it was their duty to fight for the freedom and dignity of every human being.

William Wilberforce, a British politician and devout Christian, was one of the leading abolitionists of his time. Wilberforce's personal reflections on God's word and his responsibilities in life produced not just an outward change in his conduct, but a profound change in his character and outlook.

On May 12, 1789, Wilberforce delivered his first anti-slavery speech before Parliament. He stated, "So enormous, so dreadful, so irredeemable did slavery's wickedness appear that... I from this time determined that I would never rest till I effected its abolition." This is a call to action we should all be willing to answer as Christians!

He spent more than 20 years in Parliament working to abolish the slave trade, and his efforts finally paid off in 1807 with the passage of the Act Outlawing Slavery in the British Empire.

In America, the abolitionist movement was led by figures such as Frederick Douglass, Harriet Tubman, and William Lloyd Garrison.

William Wilberforce, Frederick Douglass, Harriet Tubman, and William Lloyd Garrison were all individuals who dedicated their lives to fighting against the atrocity of slavery. They believed that every person should be free to live their lives without being oppressed by others. Their hard work and dedication led to the eventual abolition of slavery in the United Kingdom and the United States. However, the fight against slavery is far from over. In the present day, modern forms of slavery such as forced labor, human trafficking, and debt bondage are still prevalent in many parts of the world. To make matters worse, current immigration policies are undermining the work of these great abolitionists. These forms of slavery often go unnoticed and are difficult to combat, as they are often hidden from view.

William Wilberforce was a British politician who worked tirelessly to bring an end to slavery in the United Kingdom. He led the parliamentary campaign against the slave trade and was instrumental in the passage of the Slave Trade Act of 1807, which made it illegal to transport slaves across the Atlantic. Wilberforce's work continued until the passage of the Slavery Abolition Act of 1833, which abolished slavery throughout the British Empire.

Frederick Douglass was a former slave who escaped to freedom and became a leading abolitionist in the United States. He used his personal experience as a slave to speak out against the horrors of slavery and to advocate for its abolition. He was a powerful orator and writer, and his work helped to bring about the end of slavery in the United States.

Harriet Tubman was another former slave who escaped to freedom and then returned to the South to help others escape. She made numerous trips to the South, leading slaves to freedom on the Underground Railroad. Tubman's bravery and determination made her a hero to many, and she continued to fight for the rights of African Americans even after the end of slavery.

William Lloyd Garrison was an American abolitionist who founded the American Anti-Slavery Society. He was a vocal advocate for the immediate abolition of slavery and worked tirelessly to spread the message of abolitionism throughout the United States. Garrison's work helped to create a groundswell of support for the abolitionist movement and paved the way for the eventual end of slavery in the United States.

Despite the work of these great abolitionists, modern forms of servitude still exist in many parts of the world. These forms of servitude or slavery often go unnoticed and are difficult to combat, as they are often hidden from view. To make matters worse, current immigration policies are undermining the work of these great abolitionists.

Despite the tireless efforts of slave abolitionists in the 19th century, slavery continues to exist in various forms today. Some current immigration policies are undermining the work of slave abolitionists and perpetuating modern-day slavery.

For example, the United States' current immigration policies make it difficult for migrants and refugees to enter the country legally. As a result, many are forced to resort to illegal means to cross the border, making them vulnerable to human trafficking and forced labor. Moreover, the recent trend of separating families at the border has caused significant trauma and distress for both children and parents, putting them at increased risk of exploitation.

Similarly, the UK's recent changes to immigration laws have made it more challenging for victims of human trafficking to access support and services. As a result, many victims are left without the assistance they need to escape their situation and rebuild their lives.

In summary, forced labor, human trafficking, and debt bondage are serious forms of modern-day slavery that affect millions of people around the world. Despite the efforts of slave abolitionists in England and America in the 19th century, slavery continues to exist in various forms today. Current immigration policies in some countries, such as the U.S. and the U.K., can exacerbate these issues, making it essential to maintain Christian values in the fight against slavery.

"An Ending Slavery: A Call to Action for the Modern Abolitionist"

There is a call for Christians to understand people's differences and to overlook race or gender. At all times, we should be aware that Jesus Christ called for us to see each other as brothers and sisters, following Christ's teachings.

It is our duty, based on the teachings of Galatians 3:28, to accept these new believers as equals once they embrace Christianity. We cannot overcome the divisions that separate the world's populations if we cannot address our shortcomings as Christians.

By separating based on secular denomination, race, gender, and nationality, we undermine our faith. In our prejudices towards those different from us, we mirror the sentiments of the people during Jesus's time. Jesus initiated a ministry to unite the world under the banner of Christian love and compassion. For deeper insight, consider 2 Corinthians 5:20.

2 Corinthians 5:20 is a compelling verse that resonates with the essence of the Christian mission. The verse states, "Therefore, we are ambassadors for Christ, God making his appeal through us. We implore you on behalf of Christ, be reconciled to God."

This verse accentuates the role of Christians as Christ's ambassadors, appointed by God to convey the message of reconciliation to others. As ambassadors, Christians are entrusted with representing Christ and His kingdom in their worldly interactions. The verse underscores the Christian mission's urgency and significance. Christians are urged to entreat others on Christ's behalf to reconcile with God. This suggests the message's immediacy and gravitas, given the profound implications of not reconciling with God.

Moreover, this verse underscores that the Christian reconciliation message stems from God Himself: He appeals through us. This indicates that the Christian message isn't a human invention but originates in God's grace and love.

In summary, 2 Corinthians 5:20 reiterates Christians' pivotal role as Christ's ambassadors and the urgency of disseminating the reconciliation message.

Yet, we continue to cling to denominations and perpetuate racial inequality, when we should be united as Christians of diverse colors and nationalities. These principles are what the apostles of the early church sacrificed their lives for. They became martyrs for their newfound faith, laying the foundation for contemporary Christianity. Our actions mirror those that confronted the Jews, Gentiles, the Roman Empire populace, and their slaves.

Recognizing this, it becomes evident why Christianity flourished initially. The injustices permeating the world were countered by a shining example of a world predicated on love and acceptance. The early church grappled with many of the issues we face today, making the apostles' epistles to the churches continually relevant. To realize our potential as Christians, we must humble ourselves, believing in Jesus's teachings about accepting Christians as a collective and loving those yet to convert, enabling us to minister to them about the Holy Spirit's grace.

"An Ending Slavery: A Call to Action for the Modern Abolitionist"

We should not consider the Bible as purely academic knowledge, but as something that completes us and our character, equipping us for the challenges of life. As stated in scripture, 2 Timothy 3:16 is a significant verse in the Christian faith that speaks to the nature and authority of the Bible. The verse states, "All Scripture is breathed out by God and profitable for teaching, for reproof, for correction, and for training in righteousness."

The verse begins by affirming that all Scripture is breathed out by God. This indicates that the Bible isn't merely a collection of human writings; it is divinely inspired and carries the authority of God. This foundational belief shapes Christians' understanding of the Bible as a source of truth and guidance.

The verse also emphasizes the practical benefits of Scripture. It is profitable for teaching, meaning it instructs us in matters of faith and morals. It is also beneficial for reproof, convicting us of sin and wrongdoing. The Bible also aids in correction, helping us adjust our course and realign with righteousness. Lastly, it is useful for training in righteousness, guiding us to live in a way that pleases God.

Furthermore, the verse suggests that the Bible is comprehensive in its scope, addressing every aspect of human life. This makes it invaluable for Christians seeking to understand God's will for their lives and the world.

In summary, 2 Timothy 3:16 is a powerful affirmation of the Bible's authority and relevance in the Christian faith. It reminds believers of the divine origin and practical benefits of Scripture and encourages them to study and apply its teachings daily.

"But be doers of the word, and not hearers only, deceiving yourselves."

God emphasizes in James 1:22 that we are to be doers of the word, not merely hearers. The verse states, "But be doers of the word, and not hearers only, deceiving yourselves."

"Breaking the Chain: A Guide to Modern Slavery" is a study guide exploring the biblical teachings on human dignity and the abolition of modern slavery. This guide aims to help readers gain a deeper understanding of the Christian perspective on this issue and provide tools for action. Whether a Christian leader, an activist, or someone passionate about justice, this guide will equip you to combat modern slavery. As Christians, we are called to be agents of change, bringing light to darkness and hope to the hopeless. One of the most pressing challenges today is modern-day slavery. Despite its illegality worldwide, it exists, and it's time for us to act.

So, where do we begin? How can Christians lead the charge?

First, we must recognize the reality. Slavery persists in various forms globally, from forced labor to sex trafficking. It's a global issue demanding a global response.

Next, we need to educate ourselves and others. Understand the root causes like poverty, lack of education, and corruption. Recognize signs of slavery, report them, and address underlying issues.

Third, support organizations combatting slavery and assisting survivors. This includes organizations providing shelter, counseling, job training, and legal services to those freed from slavery.

Most importantly, approach this issue with love and compassion. See the enslaved not as statistics but as fellow humans made in God's image. Walk beside them, hear their stories, and offer support and encouragement.

In conclusion, we as Christians can be a powerful force against slavery. By dedicating ourselves to this cause, we can help unchain those still in bondage, bringing hope and freedom.

"Unchained: How Christians Can Lead the Charge Against Slavery"

Christians have a particularly vital role when addressing the issue of slavery, which has scourged humanity for centuries. Even today, millions remain trapped in forms of modern-day slavery. Forced labor, human trafficking, and debt bondage persist, often hidden in plain sight.

These practices exploit vulnerable individuals for others' profit. This report will examine these practices, their perpetration, how past abolitionist efforts are undermined by current immigration policies, and the importance of upholding Christian values in this fight.

The Bible offers numerous examples of God's concern for the oppressed and marginalized. Jesus, in particular, showed concern for the vulnerable, such as the poor, sick, and societal outcasts. As such,

Christians have a unique role in combatting modern-day slavery, using their faith as motivation for justice and equality for all.

In Galatians 3:28, the Apostle Paul states, "There is neither Jew nor Gentile, neither slave nor free, nor is there male and female, for you are all one in Christ Jesus." This statement, foundational in Christian theology, emphasizes that everyone is equal in God's eyes, and we are all called to love and serve one another.

Given today's societal divisions based on ethnicity, culture, class, and gender, the message of Galatians 3:28 remains relevant. The world still grapples with racial justice issues, gender inequality, and the oppression of marginalized communities.

Although slave abolitionists in the 19th century made strides, slavery continues in different forms today. This report will explore forced labor, human trafficking, and debt bondage, how modern policies undermine past abolitionist efforts, and the vital role of Christian values in this battle.

"The Abolitionist's Handbook: Strategies and Solutions for Ending Slavery"

In the 18th and 19th centuries, abolitionists in England and America worked tirelessly to bring an end to the transatlantic slave trade and to abolish slavery itself. These individuals were inspired by their Christian values, which taught them that all people were created equal in the eyes of God and that it was their duty to fight for the freedom and dignity of every human being.

William Wilberforce, a British politician and devout Christian, was one of the leading abolitionists of his time. Wilberforce's personal reflections on God's word and his responsibilities in life produced not just an outward change in his conduct, but a profound change in his character and outlook.In 1789, Wilberforce spoke his first anti-slavery speech before Parliament on May 12,1789. He said, "So enormous, so dreadful, so irredeemable did slavery's wickedness appear that.. I from this time determined that I would never rest till I effected its abolition," is a call to action we should all be willing to answer as Christians!

He spent more than 20 years in Parliament working to abolish the slave trade, and his efforts finally paid off in 1807 with the passage of the Abolition of Act Outlawing Slavery Itself in the British EmpireIn America, the abolitionist movement was led by figures such as Frederick Douglass, Harriet Tubman, and William Lloyd.William Wilberforce, Frederick Douglass, Harriet Tubman, and William Lloyd were all individuals who dedicated their lives to fighting against the atrocity of slavery. They believed that every person should be free to live their lives without being oppressed by others. Their hard work and dedication led to the eventual abolition of slavery in the United Kingdom and the United States. However, the fight against slavery is far from over. In the present day, modern forms of slavery such as forced labor, human trafficking, and debt bondage are still prevalent in many parts of the world. To make matters worse, current immigration policies are undermining the work of these great abolitionists. These forms of slavery often go unnoticed and are difficult to combat, as they are often hidden from view.

William Wilberforce was a British politician who worked tirelessly to bring an end to slavery in the United Kingdom. He led the parliamentary campaign against the slave trade and was instrumental in the passage of the Slave Trade Act of 1807, which made it illegal to transport slaves across the Atlantic. Wilberforce's work continued until the passage of the Slavery Abolition Act of 1833, which abolished slavery throughout the British Empire.

Frederick Douglass was a former slave who escaped to freedom and became a leading abolitionist in the United States. He used his personal experience as a slave to speak out against the horrors of slavery and to advocate for its abolition. He was a powerful orator and writer, and his work helped to bring about the end of slavery in the United States.

Harriet Tubman was another former slave who escaped to freedom and then returned to the South to help others escape. She made numerous trips to the South, leading slaves to freedom on the Underground Railroad. Tubman's bravery and determination made her a hero to many, and she continued to fight for the rights of African Americans even after the end of slavery.

William Lloyd Garrison was an American abolitionist who founded the American Anti-Slavery Society. He was a vocal advocate for the immediate abolition of slavery and worked tirelessly to spread the message of abolitionism throughout the United States. Garrison's work helped to create a groundswell of support for the abolitionist movement and paved the way for the eventual end of slavery in the United States.

Despite the work of these great abolitionists, modern forms of servitude still exist in many parts of the world. These forms of servitude or slavery often go unnoticed and are difficult to combat, as they are often hidden from view. To make matters worse, current immigration policies are undermining the work of these great abolitionists.

Despite the tireless efforts of slave abolitionists in the 19th century, slavery continues to exist in various forms today. In fact, some of the current immigration policies of certain countries are undermining the work of slave abolitionists and perpetuating modern-day slavery.

For example, the United States' current immigration policies make it difficult for migrants and refugees to enter the country legally. As a result, many are forced to resort to illegal means to cross the border, making them vulnerable to human trafficking and forced labor. Moreover, the recent trend of separating families at the border has caused significant trauma and distress for both children and parents, putting them at increased risk of exploitation.

Similarly, the UK's recent changes to immigration laws have made it more challenging for victims of human trafficking to access support and services. As a result, many victims are left without the assistance they need to escape their situation and rebuild their lives.

Summarized: Forced labor, human trafficking, and debt bondage are serious forms of modern-day slavery that affect millions of people around the world. Despite the efforts of slave abolitionists in England and America in the 19th century, slavery continues to exist in various forms today. The work of slave abolitionists is being undermined by current immigration policies, perpetuating modern day slavery to exist, albeit using different terminology.

"The New Underground Railroad: Rescuing Victims of Human Trafficking"

It is important to recognize that the fight against slavery is not over. Even though slavery is officially abolished in most countries, it still persists in various forms such as forced labor, human trafficking, and debt bondage. As Christians, we must continue to draw inspiration from the teachings of 1 John 4:20 and Galatians 3:28 and work towards the eradication of all forms of modern-day slavery.

In our own lives, we can also apply these principles by actively seeking out opportunities to love and serve people from different races and backgrounds. We can make a conscious effort to listen to their stories, empathize with their struggles, and work towards promoting justice and equality. By doing so, we can continue to be a force for change in our own communities and beyond. The messages of 1 John 4:20 and

Galatians 3:28 serve as a reminder of the transformative power of love and the importance of embracing all people as brothers and sisters in Christ. Through their application, we can work towards a world free of oppression, discrimination, and inequality, and towards a future where every person is valued and respected for who they are.

The fight against these forms of modern-day slavery has its roots in the work of slave abolitionists in England and the United States in the 18th and 19th centuries. Abolitionists such as William Wilberforce and Harriet Tubman were dedicated to ending the practice of slavery and worked tirelessly to raise awareness of its evils and advocate for its abolition.

Slavery in the 18th and 19th centuries is different than what is becoming a major international human rights form of injustice that violates each victim's god-given value as human beings. With the work of the slavery abolitionist making the sell of another human a crime, it leaves only criminals to be the perpetrators of these crimes against Humanity. To render the acts of these criminal organizations as a major threat to the laws and immigration policies of most developed and developing countries is what Christians should find as a priority and bring the force of a unified front by churches, law enforcement, and prosecution leaders."

"Forced labor, human trafficking, and debt bondage are all forms of modern-day slavery that continue to exist in various parts of the world. Forced labor involves individuals being coerced or forced to work against their will, often under the threat of violence or punishment. Human trafficking is the recruitment, transportation, transfer, or harboring of persons by means of threat or use of force, coercion, abduction, fraud, deception, abuse of power, or vulnerability for the purpose of exploitation. Debt bondage occurs when a person is forced to work to pay off a debt, which often accrues interest and cannot be repaid, leading to a cycle of debt and servitude. Despite the efforts of slave abolitionists in England and America, these forms of modern-day slavery persist, often in the shadows and hidden from public view. The fight against modern-day slavery is further undermined by current immigration policies, which often fail to adequately protect vulnerable individuals and may even exacerbate their vulnerability to exploitation.

As Christians, we must maintain our commitment to the values of justice, compassion, and love for all people. We must speak out against the injustices of modern-day slavery and work towards its eradication. This includes advocating for policies that protect the rights and dignity of all individuals, as well as supporting organizations that work towards the prevention, rescue, and rehabilitation of victims of modern-day slavery.

Furthermore, we must also examine our own actions and behaviors, ensuring that we are not complicit in perpetuating systems of exploitation and oppression. We must strive to live out the values of Christ, seeking to love and serve all people regardless of their race, nationality, or social status.

Christians are to be opposed to forced labor, human trafficking, and debt bondage as modern-day forms of slavery that continue to exist in various parts of the world. As Christians, we must maintain our commitment to the values of justice, compassion, and love for all people and work towards the eradication of modern-day slavery in all its forms.

Forced Labor

Forced labor, also known as labor trafficking, refers to situations where people are made to work against their will. These individuals are often held in debt bondage, where they are required to work for long hours without pay in order to repay a debt. Forced labor is a form of modern-day slavery that involves the use of coercion or deception to force people to work. Victims of forced labor are often promised jobs or better lives, only to be exploited and forced to work in harsh conditions without pay. Forced labor can occur in a variety of industries, including agriculture, manufacturing, construction, and domestic work. In other cases, they are physically forced to work through violence, intimidation, or threats.

Human Trafficking

Human trafficking involves the recruitment, transportation, and exploitation of people for the purpose of gaining a forced labor base. Human trafficking is the illegal trade of people for exploitation purposes, including forced labor, sexual exploitation, and organ trafficking. Trafficking victims may be subjected to physical and emotional abuse, as well as sexual assault. They may also be forced into prostitution, domestic servitude, or forced begging. Human trafficking is a global problem, and victims can be found in both developed and developing countries. Victims of human trafficking are often vulnerable individuals, including children, refugees, and migrants, who are tricked or forced into trafficking networks. Traffickers use a range of tactics, including deception, coercion, and violence, to control their victims and profit from their exploitation.

Debt Bondage

Debt bondage is a form of modern-day slavery that is particularly prevalent in South Asia. Debt bondage is a form of modern-day slavery in which a person is forced to work to pay off a debt. In debt bondage, individuals are forced to work to pay off a debt that they may have incurred themselves or that has been passed down through their families. Often, the debt is inflated through exorbitant interest rates, and the victims are forced to work for long hours in deplorable conditions.

They are unable to leave their place of work until the debt is paid off, which may take years or even decades. Victims of debt bondage often become trapped in a cycle of debt, working for little or no pay, and unable to leave their situation due to threats of violence or legal action. Debt bondage is prevalent in industries such as agriculture, manufacturing, and mining.

"The Fight for Freedom: Abolitionists in Action"

In the early 19th century, the world grappled with the evils of slavery. Although slavery had been common for centuries, the horrors were increasingly recognized. The slave trade was lucrative for many European countries and their colonies. Amidst this, voices emerged opposing slavery and demanding its abolition. One such voice belonged to William Wilberforce, a British politician and devout Christian who tirelessly championed the end of slavery.

Wilberforce's convictions were deeply rooted in his faith, and his passion for abolition stemmed from his belief in the inherent worth and dignity of all humans. He viewed slavery as a violation of God's will and felt it was Christians' duty to oppose it. He drew inspiration from the teachings of 1 John 4:20 and Galatians 3:28, which underscored the significance of viewing all individuals as siblings in Christ and renouncing the idea of slavery.

In 1787, Wilberforce established the Society for Effecting the Abolition of the Slave Trade. Its goals were to enlighten the public about the slave trade's cruelties and advocate for its cessation. He collaborated with abolitionists like Thomas Clarkson, Granville Sharp, and Hannah More to amass evidence and present a case against slavery.

Wilberforce's endeavors faced stiff resistance from those with stakes in the slave trade. However, he persisted, making numerous parliamentary speeches and proposing bills to abolish the slave trade. After years of effort, the Slave Trade Act was enacted in 1807, outlawing the British slave trade.

This historic act influenced global perspectives, spurring others to similar actions. In the United States, Christian leaders like Harriet Beecher Stowe, Frederick Douglass, and William Lloyd Garrison fervently advocated for slavery's abolition. Their motivations echoed the teachings of 1 John 4:20 and Galatians 3:28, pivotal in the British abolitionist movement.

Stowe was notably influenced by Uncle Tom's story, which she narrated in her renowned novel, "Uncle Tom's Cabin." The book profoundly influenced American society, heightening awareness of slavery's brutality and galvanizing many into action. Stowe's dedication was profoundly rooted in her faith, leading her to believe Christians should actively oppose slavery.

Frederick Douglass, a former slave, had an intimate understanding of slavery's horrors and was resolute in his fight against it. Viewing slavery as sinful, he felt Christians were obligated to eradicate it. Douglass utilized his exceptional oratory abilities to condemn slavery and urge fellow Christians to act.

Similarly, William Lloyd Garrison ardently sought slavery's abolition. He asserted that Christians should counteract slavery and strive for a just, equal society. Garrison initiated the American Anti-Slavery Society to enlighten the public about slavery's heinousness and press for its prohibition.

Together, these Christian leaders, among others, diligently endeavored to abolish slavery. They were motivated by 1 John 4:20 and Galatians 3:28, emphasizing the importance of treating all as siblings in Christ and disavowing slavery. Their efforts significantly contributed to ending slavery in the Western world.

Today, these Christian abolitionists' legacy persists. Their dedication to justice and their unwavering commitment to the anti-slavery cause...

In summary, 1 John 4:20 and Galatians 3:28's potent messages profoundly influenced history, especially in the battle against slavery. The biblical tenet of treating everyone as siblings in Christ, irrespective of race or societal standing, inspired figures like William Wilberforce and American abolitionists. Through their steadfastness and commitment, they facilitated momentous societal shifts, laying the groundwork for a more just and equal future.

"The New Underground Railroad: Rescuing Victims of Human Trafficking"

Human trafficking is one of the fastest-growing criminal industries in the world. It is a modern-day form of slavery that involves the exploitation of vulnerable individuals for forced labor, sexual exploitation, or other forms of exploitation. According to the International Labor Organization, there are an estimated 25 million victims of human trafficking worldwide. In this report, we will explore the issue of human trafficking from a Christian perspective and discuss the concept of the new underground railroad—a movement of individuals and organizations working to rescue victims of human trafficking and provide them with the support they need to heal and rebuild their lives.

As Christians, we are called to love our neighbors as ourselves and to care for the most vulnerable members of our society. Human trafficking is a violation of human dignity and a direct affront to God's command to love one another. It is a form of evil that must be opposed by all people of good will, especially Christians who seek to follow in the footsteps of Jesus Christ.

The concept of the new underground railroad draws inspiration from the historical underground railroad, which was a network of secret routes and safe houses used by African-American slaves to escape to freedom in the 19th century. The new underground railroad seeks to provide a similar pathway to freedom for victims of human trafficking. It involves a network of individuals and organizations who work together to identify victims of trafficking, provide them with safe places to stay, and connect them with the resources they need to recover and rebuild their lives.

The new underground railroad operates on a few key principles, which are rooted in Christian values. First and foremost, it is a movement based on compassion and love for one's neighbor. Those involved in the movement are driven by a desire to help those who are suffering and to offer them hope for a better future. They understand that the work they do is not only necessary but also a reflection of their faith in God.

Secondly, the new underground railroad is a movement that values the dignity and worth of every human being. Victims of human trafficking are often treated as commodities, their bodies and labor being bought and sold like goods. The new underground railroad seeks to restore the dignity and worth of these individuals by providing them with the support they need to heal and recover from their experiences.

Thirdly, the new underground railroad values community and collaboration. Recognizing that no single person or organization can end human trafficking alone, it relies on a network of individuals and organizations working cohesively. This community-based approach aligns with Christian values of collaboration for the common good and mutual care.

Lastly, the new underground railroad values justice and righteousness. Understanding that human trafficking represents grave injustice, those involved in the movement strive to bring traffickers to justice, advocate for preventive policies, and support victims in their pursuit of justice and healing.

While the new underground railroad isn't a panacea for human trafficking, it plays a pivotal role in the broader initiative to combat this issue. It complements overarching policy solutions addressing trafficking's root causes, such as poverty, inequality, and opportunity deficits.

In conclusion, human trafficking is a grave concern for all, especially Christians committed to Jesus Christ's teachings. The new underground railroad, inspired by Christian values of compassion, dignity, community, and justice, provides victims with a route to freedom and the necessary support for healing. By endorsing this movement and similar initiatives, Christians can embody their faith, assisting the suffering, and championing justice and righteousness.

Though the work of the new underground railroad is serious and challenging, it's also imbued with hope and inspiration. Participants are motivated by a profound sense of purpose, believing in love's capacity to surmount even the most entrenched evils. They also recognize the importance of humor and joy, essential for any endeavor aimed at a better world.

Ultimately, the new underground railroad exemplifies the human spirit's resilience and the faith-driven power to spur action and transformation. It provides a way forward for those aiming to manifest their faith in tangible ways and make a positive global impact. Through supporting such movements, Christians can contribute to a world where every individual is valued, respected, and free to realize their God-given potential.

"Today's Slave Trade: Modern-Day Abolitionists in Action"

We can see the tragedies unfolding where millions are fleeing their countries to immigrate to countries of less oppression. The most significant part of these terrible events is that corrupt governments, big cartels, and various ultra-rich business owners are exploiting the impoverished peoples of the world in their dream to find a safe haven to live their dreams of freedom.

It is a known fact that most people who try to immigrate without proper credentials are exploited in the new version of slavery. As Christians led by our morals, it should be a call to exercise our knowledge and follow Galatians 3:28, holding all persons as equals in our hearts. This is not being accomplished, and most pastors do not teach diligently on this scripture.

Why are modern forms of slavery allowed to grow and spread throughout the world? As the Devil sets the stage for his Anti-Christ to step onto the world stage, he is propagating misery into every corner of the world. But when cartels and government officials collude to open the borders and undermine the very principles of the United States and our Christian values, we are not told that slavery is the result.

They control the media, and the topic is not given much attention. The current war on Christian values and all types of normalcy is underway, and the government seems to be instigating racial secularism to prevent Christians from coming together in Christ's teachings and stopping the great misery that is spreading like wildfire throughout the world. The current status of most immigrants is illegal, leading them to be exploited and turned into modern-day equivalents of slaves.

Why are modern forms of slavery allowed to grow and spread throughout the world? Whether it is through use as drug traffickers, used in the sex trades, or charged astronomical sums to bring them to the American border where they are exploited, the government continues to build on failed immigration policies and refuses to stop the importation of a massive amount of human traffic and drugs.

It is a political hotbed, and the strings are being controlled by the United Nations and ultra-rich industrialists from countries other than the United States.

"Ending Slavery: A Call to Action for the Modern Abolitionist"

And there is a call for Christians to be understanding of people's differences and to overlook race or gender. We should always be aware that Jesus Christ called us to see each other as brothers and sisters in Christ's teachings.

We should be aware that it is our duty to follow the words of Galatians 3:28 and accept these new slaves as equals once they become Christians. We cannot overcome the divisions that separate all the populations of the world if we cannot come to terms with our inadequacies as Christians.

We undermine our faith by separation based on secular denomination, race, gender, and nationality. We are no different than the people of Jesus's time in our feelings about anyone different than us. Jesus brought a ministry to unite the world under a banner of Christian love and compassion. Follow this line of reasoning to find the truth in 2 Corinthians 5:20.

2 Corinthians 5:20 is a powerful verse that speaks to the heart of the Christian mission. The verse reads, "Therefore, we are ambassadors for Christ, God making his appeal through us. We implore you on behalf of Christ, be reconciled to God."

The verse emphasizes the role of Christians as ambassadors of Christ, commissioned by God to share the message of reconciliation with others. As ambassadors, Christians have the responsibility of representing Christ and His kingdom in all their interactions with the world. The verse also emphasizes the urgency of the Christian mission. Christians are called to implore others on behalf of Christ to be reconciled to God. This implies a sense of urgency and importance to the message being shared, as the consequences of not being reconciled to God are significant.

Furthermore, the verse highlights the source of the Christian message of reconciliation: it is God who makes His appeal through us. This means that the Christian message is not something that we have come up with on our own, but it is rooted in God's love and grace.

Overall, 2 Corinthians 5:20 reminds Christians of their important role as ambassadors of Christ and the urgency and importance of sharing the message of reconciliation with others.

Yet, we insist on having denominations and racial inequality when we should be standing together as Christians of various colors and diverse nationalities. These are the principles the apostles of the early church died for. They became martyrs for their new religion and laid the foundation of Christianity as we know it. We are guilty of the same types of actions that faced the Jews, Gentiles, people of the Roman Empire, and their slaves.

This understanding should help us see why the Christian religion was so successful in the beginning. The injustices that filled every corner of the world were given a shining example of how the world could be if only love and acceptance were allowed to prevail. In the early church, we find all the same issues that plague us now, and it is the reason why the epistles to the churches still resonate today. To become all we can be as Christians, we must humble ourselves and believe that Jesus spoke the truth about acceptance of Christians as a group and to love those yet to be converted so that we could minister to them about the grace of the Holy Spirit.

We should not consider the Bible as merely academic knowledge but as something to complete our character, equipping us for life's challenges. As stated in scripture, 2 Timothy 3:16 is a significant verse in the Christian faith that speaks to the nature and authority of the Bible. The verse states, "All Scripture is breathed out by God and profitable for teaching, for reproof, for correction, and for training in righteousness."

The verse begins by affirming that all Scripture is breathed out by God. This means the Bible isn't just a collection of human writings; it is divinely inspired and carries God's authority. This belief is foundational for Christians, as it shapes their understanding of the Bible as a source of truth and guidance.

The verse also emphasizes the practical benefits of Scripture. It is profitable for teaching, meaning it can instruct us in matters of faith and morals. It is also profitable for reproof, meaning it can convict us of sin and wrongdoing. The Bible is also profitable for correction, meaning it can help us correct our course and get back on track. Lastly, it is profitable for training in righteousness, meaning it can guide us to live in a way that pleases God

Furthermore, the verse implies that the Bible covers a comprehensive scope. It isn't limited to certain topics or themes; it speaks to every aspect of human life. This makes it a valuable resource for Christians who aim to understand God's will for their lives and the world around them.

Overall, 2 Timothy 3:16 is a powerful affirmation of the Bible's authority and relevance in the Christian faith. It reminds believers of the divine origin and practical benefits of Scripture and encourages them to study and apply its teachings in their daily lives.

"But be doers of the word, and not hearers only, deceiving yourselves."

God makes it clear in James 1:22 that we should be doers of the word, not merely hearers! James 1:22 is a verse that challenges Christians to move beyond just hearing God's word and to put it into action. The verse states, "But be doers of the word, and not hearers only, deceiving yourselves."

Get the Rest of the story at https://discoveringthedisciples.com **Breaking the Chains: A Guide for Abolishing Modern Day Slavery**